MW00527197

THE BIG APPLE BITES BACK

SHORT STORIES ABOUT LIFE IN NEW YORK CITY

ARTHUR SHAPIRO

A|M Shapiro & Associates LLC

AlM Shapiro & Associates, LLC
61 Syrah
Rancho Mirage, CA 92270

arthshapiro@gmail.com

ISBN-13: 978-0-9976181-2-9

First Edition

Produced by Hannah Forman.
Cover and Layout by Miki Hickel.

To David, Jack, and Sophie

Each of you contributed in your
own special way.

TABLE OF CONTENTS

INTRODUCTION

I have lived and/or worked in New York City my entire life. Born in Brooklyn, went to college in The Bronx (where I met and married my wife Marlene), and lived in Queens and Manhattan. While I have had little experience in getting to know Staten Island, Marlene and I loved the Ferry and got engaged on a most memorable ride to that island.

We also lived in Freehold, NJ, but I worked in The City and suffered a horrendous commute for a long time. In fact, I always worked in NYC, even when I was with a multinational company, and, to a large extent, it was known that relocation could provide a fast track for advancement. That was not the path for this kid. I did more than okay during my work life without moving from city to city.

A few years ago, we moved to the Palm Springs area of California during the pandemic. While we love it out here, we miss NYC's pace and "adventure." I guess you can take the boy out of New York, but not the New York out of the boy. Thinking about The City from the desert made me realize that my hometown is special. Sometimes crazy, sometimes nerve-wracking, often unexpected, but always exciting and fun.

This book is my attempt to capture the spirit of that place, with stories about how things occasionally go astray and how even the unexpected can enliven life there. When you're in the midst of that activity, you go with the flow and do lots of shrugging. The peculiarities were driven home to me when we moved out here and encountered the incredulous looks and questions from West Coasters—"How come you didn't move to Florida?" Answer: Too humid and too many relatives. Or "You're from NY, aren't you?" mentioned right after I said hello and nothing more. Or the combination of stares, wonder, and stage whispers: "They're from New York, you know." As though that explained everything about us: a combination of sympathy and an "ah ha" moment.

# # #

WHY IS IT CALLED THE BIG APPLE?

From the New York Public Library website:

> New York is a city of nicknames. The City That Never Sleeps, Empire City, The City So Nice They Named It Twice…and, of course, Gotham…Today let's look at the Big Apple.

> Before it became a moniker for the city, "big apple" had other meanings. Throughout the nineteenth century, the term meant "something regarded as the most significant of its kind, an object of desire and ambition." To "bet a big apple" was "to state with supreme assurance; to be absolutely confident of."

> Also: "A jazz fan remembered that musicians in the 1920s and '30s had an expression for playing the big time after gigs in one-horse towns: 'There are many apples on the tree, but when you pick New York City, you pick the Big Apple.'"

> From History.com—New York State is America's top apple grower, after the state of Washington, but

New York City's nickname has nothing to do with fruit production. In fact, the Big Apple moniker first gained popularity in connection with horseracing. Around 1920, New York City newspaper reporter John Fitz Gerald, whose beat was the track, heard African American stable hands in New Orleans say they were going to "the big Apple," a reference to New York City, whose racetracks were considered big-time venues. Fitz Gerald soon began making mention of the Big Apple in his newspaper columns. In the 1930s, jazz musicians adopted the term to indicate that New York City was home to big-league music clubs.

So, lots of reasons, but they all amount to the same thing—a place at the top of the heap—an aspirational city.

I'm not sure I totally buy that. To me, what makes NYC great, Big Apple nomenclature or not, is its place in American history. In the late 1800s and most of the 1900s, NYC was the place where immigrants landed, and it became known as the Melting Pot. Merriam-Webster: "A place where a variety of peoples, cultures, or individuals assimilate into a cohesive whole...a process of blending that often results in invigoration or novelty." I believe that the melting pot created an attitude that is a strange combination of pride, arrogance, insecurity, and "Hey, I'm wawking here."

September 11, 2001, changed the city appreciably. The arrogance, standoffishness, and many other strange attitudes melted away as New Yorkers came together. Selfishness eroded, and helpfulness emerged; antipathy gave way to caring; the mantra became, we're in this together. It lasted more than a decade and a half, with positive remnants to this day.

Then there was Covid-19. New York didn't have it worse than any other part of the country, but the urban congestion, like other densely populated areas, made the nightmare crueler. As we sat on our eight-by-ten terrace, we were again reminded of and proud of the NYC spirit. We lived on 79th Street and the East River, with many hospitals nearby. Each day at 7:00 PM, everyone stopped what they were doing, opened their windows, or stepped outside with pots and ladles, banging away, to salute the doctors, nurses, and first responders on their shift change. Maybe that happened elsewhere, I don't know, but this was the typical New Yorker's way of saying, "Up yours, Covid."

# # #

So, I loved that city and still do. But my heart and soul now belong to California in general and the Coachella Valley in particular. This book is my homage to where I grew up, got educated, became a reasonably successful businessperson, raised a family, and had the time of our lives.

A few of the stories that follow began life as short plays. That's another wonderful part of NYC: black-box theatres everywhere, playwriting classes in abundance, and the ability to snap your fingers and organize a reading. But it takes the broad reach of a book to get one's stories to a wide audience.

I hope you enjoy these tales and laugh along with me.

Arthur Shapiro
Rancho Mirage, California

PREFACE

Setting the Stage: What makes you a real New Yorker?

In researching this book, I came across an article from TimeOut, published in October 2020, titled *51 Reasons You Know You're a Real New Yorker*. The sub-headline: *If you've experienced at least 20 of the following, you're well on your way to having that coveted "real New Yorker" credibility.*

With permission from the corporation *Time Out England Limited*, this fun article nicely sets the stage for this book. Many of the "real New Yorker" descriptions you will read in this preface will appear in the short stories that follow. I have selected 34 of the 51 of them.

You can find the full article at:

https://www.timeout.com/newyork/things-to-do/
51-reasons-you-know-youre-a-real-new-yorker

From TimeOut NY:

> *Some say you become a real New Yorker after living in the city for ten years. Others say the magical moment happens when you first pronounce it "How-stun St." instead of "Hugh-stun St." or have a major celebrity sighting and could care less. One thing's for sure: If you can cross off a majority of the things on the following list, you're well on your way to achieving real New Yorker status.*
>
> *1. You can walk, talk on the phone, and hail a cab while wearing a face mask.*

2. You'd ballpark a reasonable price for a cocktail at about $18.

3. You say you're waiting "on line" instead of "in line."

4. You don't avoid eye contact with panhandlers.

5. You've returned to neighborhoods where you lived years ago and have at least five stories along the lines of "I remember when that Starbucks/Citibank/Duane Reade used to be a dive bar/credit union/Burger King."

6. You consider iconic NYC foods (Junior's Cheesecake, John's Pizza, Shake Shack burgers, etc.) to be "overrated" but are still weirdly proud that they started here.

7. You got excited the first time you saw a film crew shooting in your neighborhood again.

8. When walking through the city, you adopt a zigzagging route to avoid waiting for the lights to change to cross the street.

9. You can spot tourists over a mile away, even when they're trying hard to look like New Yorkers.

10. You jaywalk (and would never consider not jaywalking).

11. You've walked down a street lined with restaurants while vehemently complaining that there's "nothing to eat."

12. You've never been on a sightseeing bus.

13. *You've gone grocery shopping at both your corner bodega and CVS.*

14. *You are an expert at "platforming": knowing where on the train platform you need to stand to best get to your exit/transfer.*

15. *Corollary: You walk to the exact point you know the doors are going to open, also known as pre-boarding.*

16. *You can dine outside next to a garbage truck and jackhammer drill without being phased.*

17. *You know the city's best cheap date is a ferry ride.*

18. *You know that sometimes, counterintuitive as it may seem, Newark is the nearest airport.*

19. *An interborough relationship is considered long-distance.*

20. *Your entire closet is black, and that includes the face masks.*

21. *You make the cabbie take your shorter, faster way (even if, in reality, it is neither shorter nor faster).*

22. *Every time you accidentally wander into Times Square, you back away in horror as though confronted with the devil itself.*

23. *The number 100 gets shortened to "a Hun" when referring to uptown blocks, e.g., "a Hun – 81st Street."*

24. *You have hit a cab, bus or car with your umbrella when it has blocked the crosswalk.*

25. *You call fire hydrants "pumps."*

26. *You are unfazed by the combined experience of observing a gorgeous summer garden while inhaling the smell of rancid garbage.*

27. *You've fallen asleep standing up on the subway.*

28. *Even if you have nowhere to be, you're still in a rush to get there.*

29. *You pronounce it "draw," not "drawer."*

30. *You hate bikers when you're walking, cars when you're biking, and pedestrians when you're driving.*

31. *"Hey! Let me get a..." is a perfectly fine way to greet the person taking your order.*

32. *You know exactly which direction is where, no matter where you are (e.g., "I'll meet you on the northwest corner of 53rd Street").*

33. *You see a scraggly tree in a patch of dirt on a concrete median and think, "Look at that nice little park!"*

34. *You know that dollar pizza is like sex: Even when it's bad, it's still pretty good.*

CHAPTER ONE
Stuck

I will kill myself if this train doesn't start moving soon, thought Sheila. But without realizing it, she had said it out loud. The other passengers crowded around her and gave her some weird looks. She was not the least embarrassed, however, as the crowd took a step back from her. "Sorry...I'm late for an important job interview, and we've been stuck here forever." As jaded New Yorkers who had seen it all, the crowd shrugged and went back to minding their own business.

The train moved slowly at first, then picked up speed.

Thank the gods. Maybe, just maybe, she'd get there on time.

Having been out of work because of the pandemic, Sheila desperately needed this job. Twenty-five years old and living with her parents was not how she thought her life would turn out. After graduating from Parsons School of Design, she landed an Art Director spot at a prestigious ad agency. Then Covid -19 got in the way, and it was Mom and Dad's place that kept her from becoming homeless. At last, the fucking plague had lessened, and people were returning to offices, as companies started hiring again.

She clutched her portfolio of designs and sketches from her previous job, along with some great work she had done on her own while on unemployment. Despite the subway delay, she felt good about Little Moose Communications, even if the name was idiotic. And if that weren't enough, here she was going to an interview at six o'clock on a Friday night in August. Oh well, what choice did she have?

Finally, the train pulled into Franklin Street station in Tribeca. It was ten to six, and she felt confident she would make it on time until she saw the throngs of people waiting on the platform. Most were soaked from what must have been a passing thunderstorm. The humidity inside the station was palpable. It felt and smelled like she imagined the rainforest of the Amazon would.

Sheila was slender and, at five foot five, didn't look like she would be able to force her way through the crowd to the stairway. A one-time high school athlete who excelled at soccer and lacrosse, she put her head down, clutched her portfolio tightly, and with an agile shimmy and a minor push, managed to make her way to the stairs. Throngs of riders, like attacking hornets, swarmed down in the opposite direction.

What the hell? Where were they going on a stormy night?

"Excuse me," Sheila howled as she elbowed her way up the stairs, ignoring the hostile looks she received with only a determined smile. Then the crowd parted, and finally, she made it to the street.

Yet her ordeal was far from over. It had stopped raining, but the hot, humid air felt oppressive; the expensive new outfit she had bought for her pending interview was creased and disheveled. She checked her watch. A few minutes after six. Shit. She put her head down, marched on, and briefly stopped to look at a shop window to check and try to fix her appearance.

Finally, she arrived at the office building at almost ten past six, went determinedly to the elevator, and repeatedly pushed the call button. Once she had got in, a man came running through the lobby toward her, shouting, "Hold it, please!" Annoyed,

Sheila ignored him and leaned forward to push the button to her floor. The man stuck his hand out to stop the door from closing and stumbled in, almost colliding with Sheila.

"Watch it," barked Sheila.

"Sorry," the man said. "These elevators are slow, and I didn't want to miss it."

Sheila looked at her watch, then the man, and said, "I suppose if you missed the 6:10, there wouldn't be another one until... what, the 6:15?"

The man ignored her and jammed the button for his floor. Neither tall nor handsome, with a scruffy beard and rugged clothes, he projected an aura of accustomed authority.

"Hey, it looks like you're eighteen, and I'm nineteen."

Sheila glared at him.

"It's Friday night, the weekend. Smile and lighten up."

"Listen," she said. "I'm late for an important meeting. The damn subways were tied up. I practically had to run over here. I must get to... Oh, never mind."

Just then, the elevator jerked to a stop.

Sheila was close to panicking. "What's that? Why'd we stop?"

"Oh, this old thing does it all the time. No big deal." He leaned over and randomly pushed buttons. The elevator dipped a bit and started moving again. "See? This is probably the oldest in New York. They dressed it up a bit but trust me, Mr. Otis himself installed it."

"Who is Mr. Otis, and why do I care," was Sheila's sharp

reply.

"Huh? Otis as in 'Otis Elevators'…"

"I'm not interested. The last thing I need is someone hitting on me."

"Well, you got me. I'm the elevator stalker specializing in hitting on women late for meetings and… aw, forget it."

Silence hung in the elevator.

After a moment, Sheila said, "Sorry, I'm just stressed."

The elevator stopped at last. The door opened. No one got on.

"Uh oh," said the man.

"What!"

"We call this a phantom stop. Usually, when this happens, it means there's going to be a problem. Might be a good idea if we got out and used the stairs the rest of the way up."

"We're on eight. I'm not walking up ten flights. I'm already late enough."

"Are you sure?" he asked.

"Yes. Thanks for your concern. Have a good night."

"I guess I'll stick around." Then he muttered, "This ain't good."

The door closed, and the elevator moved again. After a few moments, the carrier gave a screeching sound, dropped a few feet, and stopped once more. Sheila dropped her bag and portfolio and grabbed the man's arm. "Oh, my God! What happened? Help!"

"Stay calm. I'm pretty sure we're stuck."

"Don't just stand there. Push the alarm!" She shoved him aside to press the alarm. The loud clanging noise was earsplitting. Sheila shouted, "Help! Somebody, we're stuck in here! Help!"

The man sat down on the floor.

"What are you doing?" shouted Sheila. "Help me. I gotta get out of here."

"I think we're going to be here for a while. I've gone through this before, but never when I desperately had to go to the bathroom."

"So, you're just going to sit there?"

"I warned you that this might happen."

"Spare me the 'I told you so,'" snarled Sheila. "What's this call button?"

"It's not going to do any good."

Sheila paid no attention and pressed the button.

After ringing twice, the recorded voice of an operator came through the speaker by the door. "If you wish to make a call, you must dial a '1' before the area code and number."

"The call button is supposed to dial an emergency number. They never fixed it."

Sheila pushed harder on the alarm button and held it for a few moments. The sound remained so loud that she had to stop and hold her ears. She continued to shout for help.

"Save your breath," said the man. "It's Friday. The building is probably empty by now."

"What about the super?"

"He leaves early on Friday to go to his house on Sag Harbor."

"Is this an office building or an insane asylum? Help! Somebody!"

The man got up from the floor and tried to calm Sheila. "Look," he said, "I'm going to try to pull the door open, and maybe we're close enough to a floor to climb out." He worked on the door, and slowly, it started to open. "It's between floors," he said, with a sigh. "There's not enough room to climb out."

Sheila's face turned red, contorted in horror, and she shouted again that she had to get out of there. "Stay calm," he said. "Here's what I think…"

"To hell with what you think."

Sheila opened her handbag, rummaged through it for her cell phone, and started dialing.

"That won't work in here. There's no cell service." Sheila began to sob.

The man said, "Look, let's stay calm. We'll push the alarm every few minutes. There may be someone left in the building who will hear us."

Sheila continued to sob and told him she couldn't miss the meeting. Suddenly, she had an idea. "Wait a minute. I'm here for a job interview on the 18th floor. The person I'm supposed to meet is probably still in the building." She rang the alarm again.

"Job interview?"

"Yes. Help! We're trapped in the elevator!"

The man replied, "What company is on the 18th floor?"

"What difference does it make? Either help or be quiet."

"Do you have an interview with Little Moose Communication?"

Shock registered on Sheila's face. "How do you know that?"

"You're not having a good day."

"Ya think," said Sheila, yelling. She saw his concerned face. "Listen… I've been out of work for nearly two years. I need this job. I know it's a good fit. I know it." She broke down in tears again.

The man said quietly, "Little Moose is on the nineteenth floor. You wouldn't, by any chance, have a meeting with Tom Evans?"

Sheila calmed down and stared at him quizzically. "How did you know?"

"That's me. I was late for your interview."

"I think I am going to be sick."

"Sheila, isn't it? I've forgotten your last name."

"Powers," she stuttered.

"Is that your portfolio you're holding?"

"You're going to interview me after how I've acted? Here? Now?"

"Why not? We're not going anywhere for a while. It'll take our minds off things. Especially since I have to pee so bad."

"I'm sorry for everything. I'm not usually so horrible."

"It's okay," says Tom. "Particularly under the circumstances, but tell me, is that the way you behave under pressure?"

"No. Pressure usually brings out my innovative thinking, especially when there's a problem, a challenge, or a deadline."

Tom asked for an example.

Sheila considers this for a moment. "Here we are, stuck in this awful elevator. Who knows when we will be rescued? You certainly don't want to pee on the floor, although if you did, you couldn't make this floor look or smell any worse. But it would be embarrassing for both of us."

"What do you suggest?"

"I have a bottle of water. Suppose I pour it out. Then I'll turn around, and you can, uh, use it to relieve yourself.

"That's the extent of your innovative thinking? That I should pee in a bottle?"

Sheila backtracked and muttered something about the difficult circumstances they were in.

Tom assured her it was all okay and asked to see her portfolio.

"What, now?"

"Sure," says Tom. "As I said, we're not going anywhere. Let me see it."

He looked through the pages briefly. "Good stuff. I liked your resume. We need to continue in my office."

"Yeah, if we can get out of here."

"Do you think you can handle the pressure of a start-up

agency?"

Sheila replied emphatically. "I may not have come up with the answer to this predicament, but I think I explored the options, and I'll keep trying." She started to shout again, "Help. We're stuck in here!"

Tom interrupted her, "I'll tell you what... Let's not get into that here. I need go to the bathroom." He leaned over and pushed a few buttons on the elevator panel. It started to ascend.

"What just happened? What did you do?"

Tom had a sheepish grin and shrugged.

Sheila's face turned red with anger, "Is this something you often do? Conduct interviews in a stuck elevator?"

"Sometimes. You get to see people under stress." The elevator stopped. "We're on eighteen." Tom stepped out with a shit-eating grin.

Sheila stayed inside the elevator.

"Here we are," said Tom.

Sheila stayed in the elevator and stared at Tom for a moment. "Listen, Tom, if this was a test, you failed. I don't need the job that badly, after all. Go fuck yourself!"

Sheila pushed the down button, and the door closed in Tom's face.

CHAPTER TWO

Waiting for the Sweeper — Part One: Welcome to New York

Lots of people fear living in New York City. You know the adage, "It's a great place to visit, but I wouldn't want to live there." There wasn't much choice for John Reilly and his wife, Laurie. Laurie had a great job in Cleveland at an insurance company, and when a huge promotion came along, it could only happen if she relocated. The kids were grudgingly okay with it and tried to see it as an adventure—The Big Apple. On the other hand, John was less than delighted, but since he was out of work as a copywriter, thanks to Covid-19, he didn't have much choice other than to go along.

It was a huge adjustment, the hustle and bustle; the strange combination of arrogance and rudeness mixed with friendliness and caring; the smug street smarts; the I-know-better-than-you attitudes. What the hell, thought John. Cleveland was not exactly the sticks. They could make it if they learned how to manage this new crazy city. Sooner or later, they would become as bright as the natives. In addition, John thought that the decline of the pandemic would finally change things in his favor.

John was a Midwesterner through and through. A diehard Cleveland Browns fan, tall at six feet four, with brown hair and a smile that won people over. He was 35 years old, loved Laurie, and went out of his way to protect her in their new life. After all, being tall, blond, blue-eyed, and beautiful was not that common in NYC.

The Reilly family was slowly adjusting. Laurie loved her job and was clearly on a fast track. The kids liked their school and new friends, which surprised everyone. But poor John was the caboose on this journey, trying to get acclimated to the new environment, find himself, and work. In the meantime, he had started writing a novel.

On this hot July morning, John was standing in front of his apartment house with a container of coffee, just staring into the distance. His neighbor, Frankie Scarfone, walked up to him with his own cup of coffee and greeted him warmly. They were out to move their cars since the alternate side parking rule had been suspended during the height of Covid and only recently returned.

"Morning, Frank," said John in greeting.

"Hey," replied Frank, "Call me Frankie." Frankie was the archetype New Yorker: street smart, savvy, curly hair, 45 years old, broken nose, and rugged in appearance and manner. The truth was that Frankie was a sweetheart, a helluva nice guy. That broken nose? He told everyone it was the result of a vicious bar fight, but, in reality, he had fallen off his bike at 15, and his parents never had it fixed. Besides, he felt it made him look tougher than he was.

"I enjoyed the game last night. Thanks for inviting me," said John.

"No problem. Always good to get some fresh meat. Especially a rube from the Midwest."

John laughed. "Rube or not, I cleaned you guys out."

"Yeah, beginner's luck."

"Well, I hope you invite me back."

"For sure. I want a shot at getting my money back."

"How long have you guys been playing together?"

"Couple of years," says Frankie. "Want to be a regular?"

"Oh yeah."

"Done. The guys all liked you. Besides, they figure your luck won't last forever. So, how's it going? You adjusting?"

John paused for a moment and answered, "Well, Frankie, living in the Big Apple is tough. All these..."

Frankie interrupted him. "Hold on, kid. A real New Yorker never calls it the Big Apple. That's for tourists. And it's not even called New Yawk or Manhattan. It's The City. Got it? The City."

"Got it," says John.

"So, how's The City treating you?"

"Truth be told, it's tough. We've been here a few months. Laurie's job is great, doing well. Me? Not so good. Not many openings for copywriters these days. So, my full-time job is looking for a job."

"It's tough out there," says Frankie. "There's plenty of part-time work, though."

"Yeah, but I can't bring myself to say fries with that?"

"So, it's a big adjustment, huh?"

"New York, uh, The City, is tough."

"It ain't so tough."

"For you, Frankie, maybe."

"Listen, kid, there are a few basic rules and guidelines."

"Such as?"

"Okay, pay close attention," said Frankie.

First he told John not to be taken for an out-of-towner. "Use some street smarts. You're in this big river, see, sometimes referred to as shit's creek. And there's lots of stuff in the water that can hurt you. So ya keep your eyes open for it and keep moving along. You get into the current and act like all the other fish surviving. Capice?"

John was unsure but answered, "Yeah, I think so."

"Ever hear the words to that P Diddy song?"

"I'm not a rap fan."

Frankie did a poor imitation of the rapper, singing off-key. "Welcome to New York, mothafuckas, where we don't play, and out-of-towners get got every single day."

"Keep your day job, Frankie," said John.

"Pay attention, kid. Some simple rules to keep in mind, things that will make you a real New Yawker."

"Go on."

"New York attitude. Check this out: A tourist family with three little kids standing at a corner waiting to cross in the pouring rain. Dad has a golf umbrella. A big guy walking by casually grabs dad's umbrella and tilts it down just in time to keep the kids from being soaked by taxi splash. He keeps on walking and says nothing. That's New York."

The lecture continues: "It's Sixth Avenue, not Avenue of the Americas. Where they got that, I'll never know. Oh, and it's House-ton Street, not Houston like in Texas. The best fast-food comes from a truck. Do you want great Italian food? Forget Little Italy—it's for tourists. Go to Arthur Avenue in The Bronx. If you want a Jewish deli, head for Katz's. Don't wait in line for the food, get a table. Oh, and I don't give a shit what they call it: it's still Shea Stadium to me. The FDR? It's The Drive, nothing else."

"Lotta rules, Frankie."

"No, it's fitting in and gettin' that New Yawk attitude. Most of all, this city is about transportation."

"Huh?"

"Yeah," says Frankie. "Getting around separates a native from the Bridge and Tunnel crowd."

"The what?"

"Joisey and Island people."

"Okay, keep going. I'm listening."

"Walking down the street? Eyes front, no eye contact, but you're still looking and feeling all around. And did you know that if you're in a crowd and someone bumps into you never, ever reach in to see if your wallet is still there. That's just telling the world where it is."

"Next?"

"The subway."

"Go ahead, Mr. New Yawker, man of the city, please explain it to me," John said. "I can't figure it out. Some lines are letters, and some are numbers: what the fuck? Why can't it be simple like the color lines in Chicago?"

"Ha," scoffed Frankie. "No offense, but Chicago? You call that a real city?" Frankie paused and glanced up the street.

"Another rule... Never ask for directions. They'll either tell you to fuck off or give you a twenty-minute explanation and..." He stopped in mid-sentence.

John could feel the change in Frankie, from a genteel, nice but tough guy, into a tense, coiled predator. He looked down the street and followed Frankie's gaze, and noticed an angry-looking woman, in a blue uniform and white cap with a ticket-writing machine in hand strolling down the street as though she owned it.

John asked Frankie, "Is she a traffic cop?"

"Yeah. We used to call them Meter Maids. They didn't like it, and men started doing the job, so now they're known as Traffic Enforcement Agents. Also known as pieces of shit who think they own the city. If you don't move your car on alternate side parking days, she gets off on writing a ticket. If you're not around, the next thing you know, they tow your car."

As the traffic agent approached, Frankie nudged John and, in a loud voice, said, "Lookie, lookie ... here comes Officer Crotch-ette. How's the ticket writing business?"

"Watch your mouth," said the agent.

To John, Frankie said, "Allow me to introduce the fastest ticket writer in the city. She was fast with paper and pen, but now that they have handheld devices, she walks down the street writin' and blazin.' Ain't that so Miz Meter Maid?"

She was beyond pissed. Through clenched teeth, she told him again to watch his mouth. "I don't have to take your crap.

What exactly is your problem anyway? Don't like black folks, don't like women? I'm doing my job. And you, Mister Big Mouth, better move your car."

Frankie clearly loved getting under her skin. "Yeah. Whatever. We still have a few minutes."

She glanced at her watch and warned him she'd be back. After starting to leave, she turned around and stared closely at the windshield. "You just ruined my day."

"I'm happy, but how did I do that?

"Your tag is not expired yet. Still got a month. Don't rush to renew it. It'll be my treat to write you up." She laughed as she turned and walked away. Frankie gave the finger to her back.

John said, "Why do you want to piss her off? She'll never cut you slack that way."

"Screw her," said Frankie. "She's a nasty bitch. Whether you're nice or nasty to her, she doesn't care. A few months ago, a woman was double-parked, loading her kid into the car. It was pissin' rain. Officer Crotch-ette goes up to her car and writes her up. Heartless."

"You know, having a car in the city is a pain in the ass."

"Tell me about it," says Frankie. "Too much rubber and not enough pavement."

"I drove around an hour last week looking for a spot. Who can afford a garage?"

"That's what we're here to learn, my friend," said Frankie.

"Do tell."

"Okay… It's all about alternate side parking. No parking on

this side or the other on certain days. Supposed to make it easier for the street sweeper to do its job. Ha! That is when they decide to show up."

"And…"

"So, if you got the time, the way to beat the system is to sit in your car during the time you're not supposed to park… On this side of the block, it's Monday and Thursday from 9 to 10:30. Across the street, it's Tuesday and Friday. Everyone else moves their car. Me and some of the others… wait it out and get to keep the spot."

"What if the traffic agent comes by, and you need to move?"

"So, you do. Then drive around the block a few times and come back. Although, once, Meter Maid Crotch-ette gave me a ticket anyhow. She has a cold heart, that one."

"What if the street sweeper shows up?"

"Gets a little tricky," says Frankie. "You do the dance."

"Okay…?"

"When you see him coming or hear him, you start the motor and — since this is a two-way street — you make a quick U-turn and pull in right behind him. It's like a piro-something in ballet."

"Pirouette?"

"Yeah. That too… Time to go."

As they looked at their watches and started to walk to their cars, the traffic agent approached them.

With a big grin on her face, she said, "Well, well, well… 9:02 on my watch. I presume you gentlemen are getting into your cars to move them, correct? I can give you a ticket for just 2 minutes, anyway, but... I'm feeling generous today." She raises her voice. "You have 30 seconds to move or get a ticket. And look up and down the street... there's a bunch of us here to move you all!"

"We're going. We're going," said Frankie.

"And guess what, Big Mouth? One of us will spend the next hour and a half waiting right here. So, no going around the block today."

# # #

A few days later, John was sitting in his car listening to the radio. He shut it as his wife Laurie walked up. She was holding a bag with coffee and bagels. She handed the bag to John through the window, walked to the other side, and got in.

"John, why are we doing this?" she asked him.

"What? What are we doing?"

"This. Sitting in the car. Waiting."

"I explained it to you," he said.

"But I have a day off, and I thought we could do something... not just sit here... waiting."

John tried to explain, "We're spending time together. It's relaxing."

"Relaxing? Waiting for 10:30 so we can leave the car? John, it's crazy."

John sheepishly replied, "We're beating the system."

"What are you talking about?"

"It's a Wednesday spot. Today is important... it's Tuesday. There's no alternate side-of-the-street parking on Wednesday. So, if I leave the car here today, I don't have to move it again until Thursday. I get two days. You're here for backup in case I have to use the bathroom or something, and if the sweeper or Traffic Agent comes along, you can move the car."

Exasperated, Laurie said, "Why don't we get a garage spot?"

"Are you kidding? At over $300 a month to park?"

"John, you're obsessed with this parking situation. The other day we took a cab because you didn't want to lose your parking spot."

"As soon as I find a job, we'll look into a garage."

Laurie told him that she would not sit in the car for an hour and a half and, perhaps, she should go to the office after all. "What are you going to do today?" she asked.

"Wait for the sweeper or meter maid, whichever comes first. Then send some more resumes and maybe work on the book."

"How can you waste your time just sitting in the car?"

"I do a lot of thinking."

"Bullshit, you listen to the radio and read a newspaper. You could be doing other things. Can you at least drive me to work sometimes? It takes forever on the subway to get to lower Manhattan."

"You mean downtown."

"What?"

"C'mon. It's not lower Manhattan—it's downtown. Or the Wall Street area. Not Manhattan."

"Whatever, John. But there are some days I can't deal with the subways."

"That's because you're not using subway smarts."

"What the hell are you talking about?"

John went on parroting what he had heard from Frankie about the subways. He lectured her on how she should always stand on the platform, where the doors would open right in front of the exit stairs when she exited the train. He explained that it would save time. Next, he told her not to pay attention to the mumbling over the loudspeaker if there was a problem, to do what the other passengers did.

Laurie had had it. "You're losing it, John. Since when did you become such a ... New York insider?"

"We live here now. To get by, we need to cope like the locals. We need a New York attitude."

"You have lost your mind, John Reilly! Bye, I'm going." She walked off, and John called after her.

"And, remember, getting a seat on the subway is easy. Just stand over someone who looks like they're getting off at the next stop..." Laurie was not listening.

John, to himself: "What's the use? She never listens. Still an out-of-towner."

\# \# \#

Frankie walked up to John, asked him how he was doing, and let him know that with his new chef, his restaurant was doing great. While he was 'working his ass off,' he was making money, sleeping late, and had finally decided to get a garage spot. John congratulated him on his good fortune and for no longer playing the 'waiting for the sweeper game.'

Just then, the Traffic Agent appeared.

She looked at Frankie and said, "Well, look who's here. My good friend... uh... um... I can't seem to remember the names I write on tickets. You all look alike. Anyways, good morning to you." To John, she said, "And to you too... Mister Other Guy."

Frankie and John were silent and stared at her.

She went on. "What, no wise guy remarks?" To Frankie, "Haven't seen you around. Some other agent getting your business?"

Frankie was loving this. "You and me are done, honey. I got a garage spot."

She replied, "Good for you. Now, your friend here could use a bit more smarts."

"What's the problem?" asked John.

"Check your mail lately?"

"What are you talking about?"

She smirked and told him he was nailed twice in the last few weeks. John was incredulous and told her that no one gave him a ticket.

She says, "You're right, no one did. But you forgot to smile."

"What are you talking about," asks John.

"Notice that the sweepers are coming more often lately?"

John: "So? I move when I need to. What's your problem?"

"The sweepers got cameras on them now. I hear they got some great shots of you blocking them, standing in an illegal zone, and, best of all, an illegal U-turn… Probably a hundred and fifty bucks worth of beauty shots. Do you know what that means? I'll tell you… Two of those, and there's your garage spot. Check your mail, sonny."

She walked away with a sinister cackle, looking over her shoulder as she spoke. "Gotta love technology. Have a nice day!"

Frankie said, "Careful. Technology will take your job one day."

"Think so? Ya also gotta love the civil service and the unions… especially in New Yawk."

CHAPTER THREE
Waiting for the Sweeper — Part Two: The Melting Pot

Marty Goldfarb lost his job as Chief Marketing Officer at an insurance company. It wasn't a big surprise considering that the average lifespan of a CMO is 18 months. He had held his own for almost two years. He thought, fine, I'm okay with it. Many folks are out of work these days.

His wife Colleen's business was starting to grow, and their Upper East Side apartment had no mortgage. They could get by with one income. Best of all, Marty considered his situation a way to pursue what he always dreamt of: to write the great American novel and become a successful writer.

Like many people in his building and throughout the neighborhood, Marty did not have a garage spot and parked on the street. So, each weekday morning, he sat in his car from 9:00 to 10:30, waiting for when it would be legal to park again on that side of the street until the street sweeper had passed or when there was no sign of a traffic cop. He lied to himself, thinking it was time he could spend working on his book. That rarely happened. Most mornings, Marty just listened to the radio, flipping from one station to another.

Marty was, as usual, surfing the stations on one particular day while drumming his fingers on the steering wheel and hoping Colleen would come by with coffee and maybe even a bagel.

"… so, yesterday, I get to Chicago. It was the middle of the day, and I can't get a cab. Okay, so it's cloudy

with an 80 percent chance of rain, but the Mets are here, and I got a broadcast to do. Anyway, what's with this town? Can't I get a cab to Wrigley? It ain't New York cab-wise. Live from Chi-town…hang around for this message, and we'll fill you in on the Yankee game last night…"

He flipped the dial. It came in a bit staticky.

"WNYC… Support the station you love… pledge online if you prefer… Enter to win a trip to Paris… Visit NYC.org and see all the gifts… keep us not-for-profit… get your pledges in… And, now, two-time Congressman Kusimano who is leaving New York to move to Seattle to run for a vacant seat…."

He changed the channel again, avoiding the 'hate' stations. But ended up with—

Brothers and sisters don't laugh about the confusion about the end of days. Even Heaven can make an arithmetic mistake. It's coming; it surely is. The abominations we encounter in this world are too much. Too much for Christians to endure. Too much for our Lord to countenance. We either change our ways, or the demise of Sodom and Gomorrah will be as child's play compared to what comes…

Marty had had enough and shut off the radio. Just then, Colleen walked up to the car carrying a bag with coffee and bagels. She got in the car.

Marty reached over, took out the coffee, and looked into the bag. "What kind did you get?"

Colleen replied, "The usual. Why do you always ask me that? I always buy you the same thing."

"That's boring."

"Boring?" snapped Colleen. "Anytime I pick up something else, you moan and groan about it. This is you, in a whiny little boy voice: 'Aw, Colleeeeen, you know I love an everything bagel. Why did you get pumpernickel?' Then I say, 'Don't you ever want to try something different?' And you say, 'Other than in the bedroom, not really.' Now, that, my dear Marty, is boring."

Marty decided to change the subject. He asked about the kids and if they got off to school okay. She told him about Rebecca's worry with respect to a test and trying to skip school while their son, Sean, was his usual pain in the butt self.

Hardly listening, Marty replied, "Good, what do you have going on today?"

"More orders to fill. Some new stuff came in. The apartment is getting cramped, and if the business keeps growing, we will need more space."

"What about the storage space?"

"Do you want to keep driving back and forth to Washington Heights?" asked Colleen.

"That's what we have the car for," he says.

"Sure, when you can move it." Colleen decided to change the subject. "So, did you finish rewriting the book?"

Marty told her that he was still working on it. Unhappy with his answer, Colleen asked if he had found an agent. Marty defensively answered that he had self-published a book once and could do it again. Collen scoffed and asked, "How did that go, hon?" Marty hemmed and hawed.

"Let me remind you," she said. "You, me, Mom, Dad, my sisters, your asshole brother... a few neighbors and ex-friends—thanks to you and the book—old schoolmates, thanks to Facebook... let's see... twenty copies?"

Marty sheepishly said, "Thirty-five."

"Wow, a bestseller."

"What's an agent going to do for me even if I could get one? Take 15% of what I make?"

"Based on the last book, that would be a buck and a half," said Colleen. "Marty, we need to talk to someone about your writing career. Your books are sometimes... well, a bit out there. And you need to work harder at the titles."

Getting annoyed, Marty said, "What do you mean?"

"The book you're working on, the one about people whose business careers are moving too fast...?"

"It's a business book. Do you know how careers are ruined because people peak too soon? They get moving so fast that failure catches up with them."

"Marty," says Collen, "peak too soon? And the title, 'Premature Achievement?'"

"I thought it was clever."

"Maybe you should have called it, Oops... sorry, Honey."

Marty stared at her. After a moment or two, he said, "Are your parents coming over this weekend?"

"Yes," answered Colleen. "They haven't seen the kids in a while. They're coming for dinner."

"Swell. So, I can listen to your old man's brilliant views of politics: what was wrong about Obama, the brilliance of Trump, and how that bitch Margaret Taylor Greene would make a great president. And why I am a loser. I can't wait."

"Oh, come on, he's not so bad, just a bit opinionated...."

"And judgmental, narrow-minded, bigoted, racist, and obnoxious. And those are his good traits."

"Stop. He means well. He's proud of you."

"Proud of me?" Marty could not stop himself from going off and telling her that her father had become insufferable since becoming a supervisor in the sanitation department. "He thinks his shit doesn't stink. Ha. That's funny, a garbage man who thinks his shit doesn't stink."

Colleen asked him why he and her father couldn't get along. "He gets along with my brothers-in-law."

"That's because all but two of them are Irish. Tony and I are the oddballs. Face it, Colleen, he ain't thrilled to have a Jew and an Italian in his family. I spend lots of time talking to Tony about who your father hates more... the Heeb or the Eye-talian." He continued in a mock Irish brogue. "Oh, dear girl, if your late great, great aunt Colleen McQuire — your namesake — knew you married a Jew, she'd be spinnin' in her grave. Surely would."

"He probably hates you more than Tony, I agree," said Colleen. Then burst out laughing. "Just kidding."

She smiled at him and went on. "You know that you and he

got off on the wrong foot when you first met. He doesn't appreciate Irish jokes."

"Me? I'll never forget when he asked me, 'How do you start a Jewish marathon? Roll a penny down a hill.' I thought, hey, this guy is trying to be welcoming and remove barriers, so he feels free to make an ethnic joke. I thought that was cool. But when I did one back at him, he got pissed."

"One?" Colleen said. "It was more like a barrage. Did you have to refer to an Irish seven-course meal as consisting of a baked potato and a six-pack?"

They both laughed, and Marty continued. "I must admit that I liked the Jewish mother jokes. Why don't Jewish mothers drink?"

Colleen answered, "Alcohol interferes with suffering."

Now they were really into it. Colleen said, "What's the difference between an Irish wedding and an Irish wake?" Both at the same time say, "One less drunk."

They looked at each other and smiled the way a loving couple does.

"Marty, why are we doing this?"

Marty explained the alternate side parking issue, but Colleen was not buying it. He told her that sitting in the car for an hour and a half was relaxing, in a way, and when she came by, it was just the two of them — alone time. No kids, no tumult. She looked at him silently for a moment, then mouthed the word 'bullshit.'

He continued talking about beating the system and avoiding the "Nazi" traffic cop and the importance of a Wednesday spot. He explained that $300 a month for a garage was too much money, not to mention the joy of sneaking behind the sweeper and grabbing a spot they had just moved past.

Colleen had had it. "In the first place, that spot-grabbing reminds me of whales performing at SeaWorld. Suddenly the street sweeper appears, and all of you do a short U-turn… kind of like a pirouette… around the sweeper, like falling dominoes down the block. Oh, and how about when you fell asleep waiting and got a $150 ticket? You're wasting your time when you could be doing something worthwhile, like writing your book."

"Hey, it gives me time to think."

"Nonsense and more bullshit. You're just…"

Marty interrupts her, "Go ahead and say it, I'm cheap. Right? The cheap Jew. Guess your old man's bias has rubbed off, huh?"

"Fuck you, Marty Goldfarb. That's not what I was going to say."

"What then?"

"Think about it. You're trying to reinvent yourself as a writer. You sit here at least three times a week, every week. Eighteen hours a month. Let's say $20 an hour — I know you're worth more — but let's leave it at that for a minute. That's $360 a month! There's the garage money."

"Huh," says Marty. "And where does the cash come from?"

"Well, we can always borrow from my family until…"

Marty raised his voice, "Don't go there!"

Colleen muttered okay, okay. They both sat in silence.

Marty had an idea, "Maybe you're right. Wait a minute. Your father is a hot shot garbage man… uh, sorry, sanitation supervisor. Maybe he can give us a 'get out of jail free' card, and I can park here without a ticket, with the street sweeper going around me for a change."

Colleen laughed. "Go ahead and ask him. Let me know how you make out."

Marty agreed, then asked, "You have any ideas?"

"Yes, I do. The kids go to school around 8:30, and you start your parking vigil at 9:00 for an hour and a half."

"So?" asks Marty.

"There's some peace and quiet in the morning. Time to relax, do some writing, have a decent breakfast. And, who knows, every now and then, when it's just the two of us alone in the apartment, perhaps something will come up," she said coyly.

They looked into each other's eyes and smiled.

"That would be nice," said Marty. "Very nice."

They moved closer to each other and embraced.

Just then, there was a loud tapping on the passenger side window. It was the traffic agent, known in the neighborhood as Officer Crotch-ette. "Okay, lovebirds, get a hotel room and move your damn car before I write you up."

CHAPTER FOUR
Get Off My Set

Mary O'Connor was tired. No, make that exhausted, bone weary, totally wiped out. It was a long grueling flight from Singapore. She missed the direct, non-stop, which would have taken eighteen hours to New York City, and instead ended up making lots of stops and even a plane change.

Part of her hated the traveling, the endless meetings, strange hotels, inedible meals, the leering clients, and being hit on. But, for the most part, she loved what she had accomplished. Thirty-two years old, a Yale graduate with an MBA from Stanford, she had broken the glass ceiling and become a Senior Partner at Miles Associates, a top-notch investment banking firm. It hadn't been easy with the 'frat boys' network getting in her way, the constant harassment, lewd comments, and even dislike and jealousy from the women in the firm.

Mary's personality, patience, and intelligence ultimately won the day, and she not only came to the attention of senior management with promotion after promotion until she had become the firm's star. Handling clients was much more difficult.

At five foot seven, slender, and well-dressed, Mary looked like she had come right out of the pages of Vogue. Her striking appearance, however, was accompanied by several important traits. She knew just when a situation could be resolved with either charm or flashes of her Irish temper. Her investment acumen and incredible track record made most of the Lothario clients quickly back off when they were out of line.

THE BIG APPLE BITES BACK

Those who didn't soon were looking for someone else to handle their business. The firm's leaders supported her, no doubt, because of the deals she had made.

This last trip to China was among her proudest achievements. But it was beyond grueling, and the circuitous route home didn't help. As a senior partner, Mary enjoyed all the perks the firm allowed: first class on planes and hotels, chauffeured cars, the whole deal.

Mary got in the car at JFK and promptly fell asleep on the ride to her 79th Street and East End Avenue co-op apartment. The driver woke her a block away.

"I'm sorry, Miz O'Connor, but there's a barricade across 79th Street, and they're not letting cars proceed."

"Any idea what's going on?"

"Looks like they're shooting a film or television show."

"What?" said Mary, practically shouting. "That's insane. Pull over, John, and please give me my bag. I'll walk from here. Let those assholes try to stop me."

John handed her suitcase and briefcase to Mary, who said goodbye and stormed off. She reached the barricade and walked past it and a guy with a clipboard as she determinedly headed to her home.

"Excuse me. Hold on, lady. We're shooting a film, and you can't go through," he said.

Mary ignored him and continued to walk farther beyond the barrier. "Who the hell are you, and why are you stopping me?" she growled at him.

Arrogantly and condescendingly, he replied, "I'm Joe Moore, the PA, Production Assistant on this film. You can't go through for now."

Mary glared at him and tried again.

"Stop! What's with you? Can't you see what we're doing here? Didn't you get the notice? You can't go through right now."

"What are you talking about? I live up the street."

"I'm sorry, but we locked up the street."

Mary grew angrier and said, "Locked up the street? What's going on?"

"Isn't it obvious? We're shooting on this block, and it will be a while."

"So, I'm supposed to wait for you to finish, is that it? Are you telling me I can't go home? Are you going to stop me from going to my own home? Are you fucking nuts?"

Joe replied in a raised voice, "Look, lady… we have a permit to shoot on this street. We let everyone here know we have a long take and will be locking up the street for a couple of hours, maybe more. We'll buy you lunch. Pick a great restaurant and return later."

Mary raised her voice as well. "Are you joking? Long take… lock up the street… what the hell are you talking about? I live up the street at 515 and just returned from an exhausting trip to Asia. I'm exhausted. I want to go home and take a long, hot shower. A nap. Some business calls. Now, as to your movie or TV show, please get out of my way."

"Hold on. Listen to me. I'm telling you, it's dangerous to walk on the set right now."

"'Set?' That's my street, you idiot! I live here and don't give a shit about your filming."

"We're setting up for an explosion scene, and the last thing we need is for a civilian to get hurt. For your safety, get something to eat and return later. This is an important shot. Please! Expensive, too, I might add."

Mary was beside herself with anger. "I'm going to try again. You listen to me closely, Hollywood Boy. Long, hard trip from Asia... me tired... need shower... need nap... must make a business call... real business, not show business... no want to eat... no want to wait. You... kiss my ass and get the hell out of the way!"

Joe replied in a whiny, schoolboy voice, "This is an important scene. It costs a fortune. We can't stop it... It's not my problem that you missed the notice to stay indoors or stay away..."

Mary interrupted, "Stay indoors or stay away? Who the hell do you people think you are? What you're doing is make-believe. What I'm doing is real life."

Joe replies pompously. "This will be a blockbuster film. You'll tell all your friends that it was filmed on your street when it comes out. Trust me: you'll be saying things like, 'Look, there's my building.'"

"You self-important little schmuck. I'm more likely to say, "That's the film where I beat the shit out of the jerk who wouldn't let me go home!"

"Do you realize you just threatened me? There's a police officer at the end of the block. Should I call him?"

Mary looked down the street, and a big smile came to her face. "Sure. Call him. Film or no film, explosion, or no explosion, long take, locked up the street, open street... whatever... you can't stop me from going to my home."

"Do you know how much money, jobs, and other benefits the film industry gives New York City? Why can't people like you understand? People in LA get it — why can't you people?"

Mary snapped back at him. "What? Are you providing jobs and other benefits? So why are you using a caterer rather than getting food from the neighborhood? What benefits? Keeping me from my home is benefitting you, not me."

"Oh, that's enough, Miz New Yawker. I knew this city would be a problem."

"Well, I suppose in the land of sham—also known as La-La land —they're much hipper than New Yorkers. Listen, I'm not going to debate the merits of the film industry in New York with you. I... am...simply...going...to...my...home. Now..."

Mary went around the barricade with renewed vigor, and PA Joe put his hand up in a 'stop' motion. In so doing, his hand landed on Mary's shoulder. "How dare you touch me?" She stopped, looked at him, and punched him in the nose.

Joe was wailing and crying. "She hit me! You hit me. I can't believe you hit me! Oh, my nose is bleeding. Call the police!" he said to no one in particular. "Arrest this crazy woman!"

Mary replied sheepishly, "You hit me first."

Hearing the shouting and the tumult, the Assistant Director ran over to Mary and the P.A. "What's going on? What's wrong with your nose, kid?"

"I tried to keep her off the set. I reasoned with her, then she suddenly hauled off and punched me in the nose. Is it broken? Will I need new headshots?"

"You are lying, you little shit," said Mary.

"What's this all about?" asked the AD.

Joe tried to explain further, but Mary cut him off. "I'm trying to get home. I've been traveling for over 24 hours from Asia, and I want to go upstairs to my apartment, shower, and sleep. Oliver Stone here wouldn't let me through. He pushed me, and I felt threatened, so I punched him.

"I didn't mean to push her," whined the P.A.

The Assistant Director weighed in, "Ma'am, my name is Jason Lynch, and I'm the assistant director of this film. I'm truly sorry for your inconvenience... but will you give me a few minutes to straighten things out and get you home as soon as possible? Please. It won't take long."

Mary agreed and asked him to hurry. He turned to the P.A. and asked him to step aside with him so they could talk and resolve the matter.

His first words to Joe were, "Are you out of your mind?"

"What's wrong?" he said.

"What's wrong? asked Jason. "What's your name again?"

"Joe, uh, Joe Moore."

"Well, Mr. Moore... in the first place, permits or no permits, you can't keep people off the street, especially if they live on the 'set.' In the second place, genius, try a little kindness and charm."

Joe tried to explain further and was interrupted by Jason. "Shut up. Third, if being polite doesn't work, call the cop we hired for help. A badge sometimes does the trick."

"But he's at the other end of the block."

"That's what the radio is for, you moron. Let's try to reason with her. I only have ten minutes before the next take."

They walked back to Mary, and just then, the police officer appeared. As he approached them, Joe spoke to Jason in a low voice, "Here's the rent-a-cop now." Mary heard him and was livid.

The Police Officer said, "Hello, gentlemen, what's going on? I could hear the shouting at the other end of the street." He looked at Mary and broke out with a huge grin. "Oh, hi Mary, when did you get back?"

"Hi, Uncle Mike. Just got back."

The P.A. Joe and the A.D. Jason said simultaneously, "You know each other?" The P.A. added, "Uncle Mike?"

Mike said, "Sure, that's my niece, Mary. My kid brother's daughter. An investment banker. Pride of the family. So, what's up?"

"Let me introduce you to my new friends," says Mary. And points to the P.A. "This little shite is a hot shot movie something-or-other." And to the A.D., "And this is his boss... must be a super-hot shot." To the P.A., she says, "This is Mike O'Connor, one of the most decorated police officers in New

York City. Despite his accomplishments, the city pays him squat, so he must moonlight for dickheads like you."

"All right, Mary. That's enough. What's going on here?"

The Assistant Director replies, "Just a misunderstanding."

"Just a misunderstanding?" says Mary. "I just want to go home."

"And you will," says Jason. "When it's safe."

"When is that?" asks Mary.

Uncle Mike answers, "Mary, they got this explosion scene, and it just ain't safe. They let everyone know, and I thought of you, but you were away, and well, you got back sooner than I expected."

"We can put you in a hotel for the night," Jason said. "We'll have a limo here in a few minutes if you say okay, then a suite at the Peninsula. Back in your bed tomorrow. I'm sorry about all this. Truly I am."

Mike says, "If you prefer. Your Aunt Grace and I would love to have you stay with us tonight."

Mary turns to Jason and asks, "How much longer until the scene ends? I want my own home and bed. Thanks anyway, Uncle Mike."

Jason jumps in, "Tell you what… give me an hour, two at the most, and no matter what, you go home. In the meantime, you can use that trailer over there to rest up. What do you say?"

Mary replies, "Okay, Jason, is that your name?"

"Yes, Jason Lynch."

"I'm so tired. I want to crash."

"I understand. Asia to LA is tough. To New York, it must be tougher. Go rest. I'll get you out of here as soon as I can. Promise."

"Okay, whatever you say, Jason. Just one favor."

"Sure."

"This dumb shit, whatever you call him…"

"Production Assistant," says Jason.

"Right. Can I kick him in the balls?"

"Whatever you like."

Joe chimed in, "What?"

"Oh, never mind," said Mary. "I'm too tired."

"Mr. Moore, get outta here and tell whoever got you this gig that I said hi… and goodbye."

"This ain't over," whined Joe.

"Oh, yes, it is," said Jason.

He turned to Mary as Joe slunk off. "Mary, I must go. Limo and stay the night at the Peninsula? Or wait an hour or two and off to your place?"

"Peninsula, I guess. I'm already packed," she smiled at him.

"Good choice. The car will be here in a few minutes. I'll have someone take you there and get you settled."

"Thanks," said Mary.

"We aren't all so bad."

"I see that," replied Mary.

Jason said, "Can I buy you lunch tomorrow?"

"I'd like that."

"Uh oh," said Mike. "Could be the start of…"

Mary cut him off. "Uncle Mike, please be quiet."

Mike, laughing, managed, "Is that how you talk to me? My niece."

Ignoring him, she said, "Call me tomorrow."

Jason said, "I will." He turned and yelled to the team, "Let's go, people. We're losing the light."

CHAPTER FIVE
The Pushcart Part One: The Irish Sweepstakes

Max and Minnie Shpire are poor and living from hand to mouth in a lower-middle-class neighborhood in East New York Brooklyn, NY. A community made up of Jews, Italians, Irish, Blacks, and Latinos, an NYC melting pot.

Their home is a three-story walk-up apartment around the corner from Max's business. The apartment is small and, with three kids, a bit cramped. The two boys, Shelly (also known as Shia), the older one, and Archie, the youngest, share one bedroom. The oldest child, Dolores, sleeps on a pullout bed in the living room. All the kids are expected to work at the business, starting at a young age.

Max and Minnie came to the U.S. from Eastern Europe as teenagers around the end of the First World War. Both dreamt of attaining the "American Dream," which for three decades eluded them. Max is short at five feet seven inches but tough and wiry with a streetwise savvy. He dreams of growing his business, learning new things, and enjoying his life. Minnie has one simple (but virtually unattainable) dream: to become wealthy and change their lives by winning the Irish Sweepstakes. Winning the Sweepstakes is a dream for Minnie, if not an obsession, and she buys tickets regularly.

The Irish Sweepstakes, also known as the Irish Hospitals' Sweepstakes, one of the largest lotteries promoted internationally, was authorized by the Irish government in 1930 to benefit Irish hospitals. It is extremely popular in these pre-lottery days in the USA. During the five plus decades of its existence, the contest has received more money from the United States than any other country, although all the tickets sold here are smuggled in and sold illegally.

Ticket stubs are returned to Ireland to be drawn from a barrel and matched with the name of a horse running in a significant Irish or British race. The largest prizes go to ticket holders whose horses won, placed, or showed. It is basically a lottery.

Popular among poor, working-class families trying to reach for a lifeline to change their standard of living, the 'grand jackpot' is an obsession but also a challenge. One needs to know whom to buy from to avoid counterfeit tickets, pray for a win and check the papers daily during the event. It is also not unusual for the person who sold a winning ticket to alert the holder via phone or telegram.

# # #

Max has a stand in an "open-air market," licensed by the city, which means he has a designated spot, and there are roughly 25 other vendors. The people in the neighborhood refer to the stand as a "pushcart," mainly because the owners store their stand/cart overnight in nearby garages and the carts themselves were reminiscent of those used to walk the streets.

The vendors are pushcart peddlers, and their only goods for sale are fruits and vegetables. Imagine three avenue blocks full of these stands, all competing with one another. Rounding out the market picture are all sorts of stores, including butchers and fish stores (some catering to Jews and some to Italians), clothing, hardware, groceries, and luncheonettes (as they are called). Assorted others round out the picture on Blake Avenue

Outdoor Market.

The pushcart peddlers are a breed unto themselves. Unencumbered by rent and other store overhead, they manage to scrape out a living. But the downside, of course, is that they can't work in inclement weather. Rain, snow, and freezing cold keep the customers away from the outside stands. The peddlers cannot pull out their wagons, are concerned about their produce, and can't work.

The decision to not open on some days is challenging since the weather can be bleak in the morning and clear up later. In those instances, the men go to one of the luncheonettes, drink coffee, eat eggs or pastries, and hope the weather improves that day. A missed day not only leads to a loss of income but also jeopardizes the freshness of the produce.

The peddlers are a rough bunch of men, in some ways analogous to longshoremen and other formidable characters in the 1950s. Operating on the street, they are exposed to petty thieves, bookies, loan sharks, corrupt cops, and other unpleasant people. As a result, despite their fierce competition, a strange sort of comradery exists. It shows with banter about each other's failings, telling honest and made-up stories, assigning nicknames, and lots of practical jokes.

On a cold, below-freezing day in January, the peddlers assemble in Stern's Candy Store and Luncheonette and wait for the weather to improve.

While busy talking and poking fun at each other, in walks Red Levine, also known as Penicillin. He got that name by selling week-old cauliflower, which had developed mold. Max, whose stand was next to Red Levine, saw the cauliflower and asked him if he was making penicillin from the mold. The name stuck, and they hated each other from that day on. Red kept infringing on Max's space, which led to many unpleasant encounters. Red's real name was Alvin, as in Alvin and the Chipmunks, a popular animated rock band. Max refers to him as Alvin the Cheap Monk, thereby adding to the animosity between them.

Red Levine is a big man, around six foot five, with flaming red hair and a pot belly that looks like he swallowed a watermelon whole. He barges into the luncheonette and immediately glares at Max. "Look who's here...Maxie the Taxi...whatsamatter Maxie, the cold too much for your old bones?"

Max is half his size—length and width—but wiry, muscular, and fearless. He is known as a guy you don't mess with in the neighborhood. The story about him is that a local hood was shaking him down one day after the war. It started when the gangster would buy tons of fruit and tell Max to put it on his tab, which he never paid. At first, Max went along and figured the free fruit was a small price to avoid a hassle. But things escalated. The hood began pestering and then threatening Max for "protection" money. When Max asked what he would be protected from, the hood said, "Me."

He refused to pay, and things escalated with threats and damage to his pushcart. One day a car drove up on the street side of the stand, and three guys got out. The gangster who harassed Max walked over to him, reached into his jacket pocket, and withdrew a mean-looking blackjack. Max calmly and nonchalantly reached into the cart and pulled out a large hammer he used to open fruit and vegetable boxes. He slowly walked over to the gangster and, without saying a word, hit him smack on the head. The hood was now the proud owner of what would become a sixteen stitches gap in his skull. His knees buckled, and he fell to the ground. It was over in a flash.

Turning to the gangster's buddies, Max said, "You better take him to the hospital, I'm sure he has a concussion." As they took him away, they glared at Max threateningly. To which he responded, "If I ever see you around here again, you'll get the same." They put the hood in the car and quickly drove off.

How Max managed to avoid getting killed added to his mystique. Some rumored that he made a deal with the boss gangster to keep his hoods away. Others believed that Max knew some bigshots at Murder Incorporated who managed to resolve the problem. Either way, Max became the hero of the neighborhood and a man not to be messed with.

For Red to get in Max's face, therefore, is seen by the other men in the luncheonette as a supreme act of courage. But Max is not the type to look for trouble or get into a fight. He shrugs, smiles, and continues drinking his coffee and eating his fried egg on a roll. Max's motto was "Don't get mad. Get even."

Red turns to the group in the luncheonette and, in his booming—some would say loud-mouthed—voice, asks, "Anyone seen Morty? I'm feeling lucky and need some tickets."

Morty was the neighborhood Irish Sweepstakes dealer. He had been selling them since before the war, hardly had any winners but kept doing business because everyone felt he was honest... The tickets were not counterfeit. Or, at least, no one could prove otherwise.

Morris the Mouth pipes up. "Saw him at Nellies, selling his no-win sweepstake tickets."

Without another word, Red bolts from the luncheonette.

Max and the three other peddlers in the booth with him look at one other. Stretch spoke up first, "That fat piece of shit has some nerve... storms in, shouts like he owns the joint, insults Max, and thinks we're his secretary. I hate that guy!" The others chime in with complaints about Red, but Max just keeps quiet. "Why so quiet, Max," they all want to know.

"There's no point arguing with that louse. Here's a man who sells close to rotten stuff, then argues with the customers who bring it back. He's giving all of Blake Avenue a bad name... he's not worth the trouble."

"I guess," says Sam, "but I sure would like to teach him a lesson."

They all get quiet for a while. Suddenly, Max starts to laugh.

# # #

Max and Minnie live around the corner from Max's pushcart location. Max often goes home for lunch, and Minnie looks after the pushcart and the customers.

They are an interesting couple who emigrated to America around WWI. Minnie, aged 18 at the time, came just as the war started and managed to escape with almost her entire family. She grew up in a city called Lodz, which was part of Poland, then Russia, and now who knows? Her father was a venerable Hebrew School teacher who placed a premium on education and raised his family with those values.

Max came to America right after the war, at age 20. His father, Louis, left before the war to come to America and work until he had enough money to bring the whole family over. Unfortunately, the war interfered with his plans, and he had to wait for the war's end for his family to join him. Max was not a bit concerned. He was a teenager who knew how to ride a horse and shoot and, while he managed to avoid conscription in the Russian army, he did become a foot soldier for the Bolsheviks. With his father gone, he had to act as the head of the family and care for his older sisters and younger brother. At five foot seven and slight in build, he was nonetheless courageous and tough.

Minnie and Max met in the early 1920s in Brownsville, Brooklyn, when Max worked at his father's pushcart. Minnie was a customer. Their relationship deepened when they found themselves learning English and getting a high school diploma in the same classes.

Minnie's upbringing was sometimes a source of disagreement among them. She was raised religiously and taught the importance of education and 'upward' mobility. While she never said it out loud, she always felt that Max could do better, and maybe, just maybe, if you pushed him hard enough, he might become what she wanted him to be. Max was a dreamer and often chased his dreams to Minnie's consternation and eventual interference. His ambition was to be a leader in his Lodge and to improve his photography skills. Perhaps he saw photography as a way to shut Minnie up by improving their standard of living. But he was serious about it beyond the economic value and went to night school to learn the craft. Part of the garage where he kept the pushcart was converted into a dark room.

By the time they approached their 25th anniversary, Minnie had begun to change. Quite possibly, the difficulty with the birth of her youngest child caused some chemical imbalance, or perhaps it was what Minnie often referred to as a "change of life." When the children became adults in later years, they felt she might have been bipolar.

The relationship with Max went from unreasonable to irrational. She interfered in his business regularly, bemoaned her station in life in a passive-aggressive way, accused him of having an affair with the Lodge's secretary, and much more. They fought often.

Divorce was not in their vocabulary, so they stuck it out. Their moments of joy and happiness became fewer and farther between.

# # #

In May of that year, the sweepstakes was held in Ireland. Ticket stubs from the US have been returned to be drawn from a barrel and matched with the name of a horse running in a major race. On the same day in May, it is pouring on Blake Avenue. The pushcart peddlers watch the downpour from Stern's Luncheonette.

Red Levine bursts into the store soaking wet and, with a shit-eating grin on his face, sits on a counter stool, waves a ticket stub, and announces, "Hey losers...this is it. The winning ticket." Someone in the crowd yells, "How do you know? Did one of your rotten, poisonous tomatoes tell you?" They all laugh, and someone else, sitting in the booth with Max, yells, "Don't be silly. It was the talking eggplant just before it died from mold."

"Very funny. Assholes. I know it's a winner because... I know it. You can all kiss my ass as I walk away from Blake Avenue and you clowns." Red turns his stool around and waves at the waitress to bring him coffee.

Fifteen minutes later, Red finishes his coffee and, with a middle finger salute, leaves the luncheonette.

Max says to his friends, "What a putz. How does he know he's going to win? He knows." He lowers his voice. "I have been waiting for this. It's just perfect. Know what I'm going to do? I'm going to send a telegram to that shmuck—'Red (stop) Your number in the sweepstakes came up a winner (stop) Hundred large (stop) Call me to get details (stop) Morty (end)'"

The others look at each other and laugh. "But what if he calls Morty and finds out it's a hoax?" The others agree.

"I guess you gents haven't heard. That's the beautiful part. You know the secretary at the lodge?" They all nod. "Well, she's a good friend of Morty's wife. It turns out Morty had a stroke and is in rehab in the Catskills. His cousin Sy has taken over the 'Business,' and no one is supposed to know until the next sweepstakes. She's also a good friend of my sister Pauline and told this to her and Pauline told me. Good luck to Red trying to find Morty, thinking he won big but can't get ahold of him."

"He'll find out sooner or later," one of the guys says. "Sure," says Max, "But a few days of that fat slob going crazy will be fun to watch."

Max goes off to send the telegram.

# # #

The next day is bright and sunny. The rain was totally gone, and since it was a Thursday and a very busy shopping day on Blake Avenue, with everything closed the day before due to the weather, the shoppers are out in force. The peddlers are as busy as if it were Easter or Passover.

Around the corner, at Max and Minnie's apartment, the phone rings. It is a not-too-bright person who has hurriedly announced that he is from Western Union and has a telegram. They want to send it over and call to be sure someone is at home.

Minnie is concerned. A telegram is not good, especially when they call to tell you they are coming by. In her experience, most telegrams are for congratulations. They had gotten many when they were first married. Other telegrams meant trouble.

Twenty minutes later, there is a knock at the door, and a Western Union delivery person hands Minnie the telegram. While he waits patiently, presumably for a tip, Minnie ignores him, tears open the envelope and closes the door.

She reads it quickly and only sees the first sentence: "Your number in the sweepstakes came up a winner." She nearly faints. Her head is reeling from shock and happiness. Could it be that it had all come to pass after so many years, prayers, and dreams? Their life of what she thinks of as squalor is now behind them.

She runs next door to the Lipton's and knocks on their door. When Miriam opens, Minnie decides to keep her composure and her good fortune to herself. "Hi, Minnie. What's going on?"

"Nothing much," says Minnie, "I need a small favor."

"Sure, what is it?"

"Can you watch Archie for a while? I need to go around the corner and help Max. Maybe he can come in and watch Howdie Doodie?"

"Sure, no problem. He's a pleasure."

Thanking her profusely, Minnie returns to the apartment, removes her smock, grabs Archie and a toy or two, and hands them to Miriam Lipton. She runs down the staircase with uncharacteristic speed and joy, heading around the corner to Blake Avenue.

One of the interesting things about the Blake Avenue Market is that the side of Blake Avenue that the pushcarts are on changes once a year. They move to the shady side in the spring/summer and the sunny side in the fall/winter. That means that Minnie could walk/run to the pushcart without crossing the street in heavy traffic.

She breathlessly arrives at the stand and shouts, "Max, close up, put the pushcart away…you won't need it anymore. I have great news!"

"Calm down. Whatever it is, all of Blake Avenue doesn't need to know. Come back here."

Minnie goes around the pushcart to the street side, and she whispers to Max, "We won! All these years, you laughed at me for buying sweepstakes tickets… wasting money, you said. Well, Mister. We won the Irish Sweepstakes!"

Nervously, Max says, "How do you know?"

"I got a telegram."

"Do you have the ticket?"

"Someplace at home."

"Let me see the telegram."

After a moment, Max's face turns white.

"Did you read this carefully, Minnie?"

"What's to read? It says we won."

"Um...it...uh, it says that the telegram is not deliverable and is being sent back to the sender."

"What are you talking about?"

"Look, Minnie, you know how we all hate Red Levine, you included?"

"So, what does that have to do with it?"

Max is looking down at the ground. "Well, a few of us decided to trick him and send a fake telegram that he won the sweepstakes and needs to find Morty to collect. Except that Morty isn't around."

"A few of you? It seems to me that you were the fool who did it and stupidly left your home address."

"And you didn't notice the return to sender stamp. All you thought about was winning the big prize."

Minnie walks off in a huff with a facial expression that reads, I'll get even.

That night, after a cold dinner of canned tuna fish, Max

musters up the courage to ask Minnie, "Okay, the trick back-fired on me. I'm sorry. But can you show me the tickets you bought? Who knows, maybe this crazy thing has a happy ending?"

Minnie looks down and has a combination of a smile and a frown. She says sheepishly, "I forgot to buy one this time."

They look at each other and laugh hysterically for the first time in years.

CHAPTER SIX
The Pushcart — Part Two: The City Dump

Max and Minnie Shpire live on Warwick Street in the easternmost section of Brooklyn, known as East New York. It's a step up from where they previously lived, Brownsville, Brooklyn, home of gangs like the Amboy Street Dukes, Murder Incorporated, and other sketchy people.

But East New York is only a small step up with its up-and-coming wannabe hoodlums like the Triangle Gang, who hang out on the triangle block between New Lots Avenue and Livonia Street. Unlike their Brownsville counterparts, who are stupidly fearless, the East New York bums are either more brilliant or more cautious.

Brownsville's open-air markets (also known as pushcarts) are constantly the target of shakedowns and extortion. But the markets in East New York have no such problem. The push-cart peddlers there are tough, no-nonsense men, and dangerous to mess with. The most notorious and threatening is Max Shpire. A legendary figure who took on gangsters and won, Max was calm and friendly on the outside but very volatile when pushed or challenged. It is remarkable since Max is five foot eight, with a slight build, and very slender. But when angered, Max always turns from docile and pleasant into someone to be avoided. His assumed but probably invented friendship with Bugsy Siegel adds to his mystique.

His fearlessness stems from his teenage years in western Russia and eastern Ukraine. He is never sure because, during WWI, the borders kept changing. His father left in 1916 to come to America and earn enough money to bring the family over—three daughters and two sons—Max being the oldest. The war took a turn, and the Russian Revolution began with the Bolsheviks, later known as Communists, deposing the Czar. They needed local support, and Max, who could give a shit about politics, found himself at sixteen as their local champion. They gave him a horse and a gun and told him he was in charge of his town. The fact that the horse stepped on his foot, breaking a toe, and he was eventually attacked by a guard dog—leaving a scar he was proud of his whole life—only reinforced his personality and grit. Max organized the journey and assured their safe passage when his father finally sent enough money to bring the family over.

Minnie's background is far less dramatic. Her father was a teacher, and they enjoyed a pleasant life in Russia until the war broke out. Like Max, someone from the family—her oldest brother—came to America and earned enough money to bring the family over. Minnie is an attractive, slender woman with a figure most other women compliment. Her sole "flaw," so to speak, was slight buck teeth.

Her personality and demeanor are an enigma. Warm and loving one moment, she could turn to the opposite in a second. Family quarrels and conflicts always seem to follow her, primarily of her instigation. And her immediate family is not immune from her wrath and anger. She and Max often quarrel over money, imagined slights, and why he can't be more than a peddler in an NYC open-air market. Their children are also occasionally the focus of her wrath.

In 1955, when the Brooklyn Dodgers finally won the World Series, Max and Minnie had three kids. Dolores (sometimes called Dorothy), 23, Sheldon (called Shia), 19, and Arthur (known as Archie) is the youngest at 11. They are expected to help and work with Max at the pushcart. Therein lies our story.

# # #

As the oldest, Dolores was the most frequent worker in the family until Archie was old enough to help. She was the apple of Max's eye, and Max often said, "I'd rather have one daughter than a dozen sons." Archie was sure he was not part of the wish and figured that Shia was the target. When Archie was eight and eager to grow up, he started to work at the pushcart and loved the responsibility and maturity that came with it. Shia, at 16, seized the moment and was only too happy to pass the baton to his younger brother while he went off doing what teenagers prefer to do.

Shia's absences have been okay with Max who feels that Shia's mind is elsewhere, and Archie, even at the age he is, is a hard, focused worker. It isn't okay with Minnie because Shia only wants to go where there are kids with more affluence and more enjoyable social lives. He spends most of his free time in Crown Heights, where he hopes to be accepted by the rich kids. It drives Minnie crazy, and despite her upward mobility aspirations, she continually begrudges her older son from doing the same.

The relationship between Dolores and Minnie could be better too. Dolores, as a teen, wanted a college education. But, at the same time, she wanted fashionable and expensive clothes. For her part, Minnie gave her a choice, clothes, or college. They had numerous arguments, which only add to the tension in their home.

By 1955, things have settled down a bit in the Shpire household. Shia, known to his friends as Shelly, has started college in NYC by this time. The deal made with his father is that he would get help with tuition—as a free university, the city colleges charged very little—and an allowance if he agrees to work at the pushcart on Sundays, the busiest day of the week.

Dolores has gone in a different direction and taken a job in the garment center, probably closer to the clothes and fashions she covets. More importantly, she has married her childhood sweetheart, Maury, whom she has known from her early teens. While they have always planned to marry, the Korean War and Maury's drafting into the Army have sped up the timing. As a married woman with a job, her days at the pushcart are behind her, even though she had lived with Max and Minnie until Maury came home.

Minnie has eased off the pressure on Dolores, even if she is not pleased that she has married a husband who is in a war zone. As a married woman, Dolores might have a family soon, and Minnie relishes grandparenthood. And she is working and contributes to the household expenses.

So gradually, a calmness fell over the Shpire household, at least temporarily.

# # #

Passover and Easter are the busiest times of the year for the fruit and vegetable peddlers on Blake Avenue in East New York, Brooklyn. If they come around on different calendar dates, it is a bonanza: two bites of the apple. Those celebrating Easter are the better customers. They buy more, especially vegetables, and rarely bargain. The Jewish shoppers, on the other hand, whether by the nature of their personalities or because the pushcart owners are also Jewish, are thorough hagglers and bargain hunters. But Passover is unique, and the nicest customers get the best produce and occasionally a discount.

In the spring of 1955, both Passover and Easter fall within three days of each other. Easter Sunday is on April 10th, and pre-and post-Church, the Christian—primarily Catholic—shoppers are out in force, buying produce for the holiday dinner. The pushcart market is closed on Saturday for the Jewish sabbath since the neighborhood is mainly Jewish. So, for anyone who wants fresh food, Sunday is the day.

This year Passover is on April 13th, the following Wednesday, with a few days of intense preparation for the Jewish shoppers, which means that Sunday is the best day to get the shopping out of the way. It is a "perfect storm."

Max is ecstatic. It means that this Sunday will be his busiest of the year. With any luck, he can pay off the new Plymouth he bought. He informs the family that it is "all hands on deck" for that Sunday. Minnie, Dolores, and Archie are enlisted to show up at eight in the morning. But Shelly, the best at schmoozing customers, informs the family that he has a hot date the prior Saturday night and isn't sure he could make it on Sunday. Minnie informs Shia that she will throw him out of the house if he isn't there at the start of the day. He smirks, looks her in the eye, and knows she means it. She said, "If you don't help out tomorrow, you are gone from this family, and I will sit Shiva for you." Shiva—the time after someone has passed away—is rarely applied to the living except in a dire situation. Shia caves in and agrees to be there.

So, there they are, the entire Shpire family, ready to conquer Blake Avenue on this busy day.

Max is hardworking and gets up most weekdays at 4:30 to go to the wholesale market and get the best produce. But he isn't especially good at financial or business matters. His focus is on the quality of what he bought. There is no cash register when customers pay him at the pushcart. He puts the coins in a cigar box and the bills in his pockets. When he buys work pants, he either purchases those with deep and reinforced pockets or takes them to a tailor to fix them to hold the bills. But he is pleased with his system: dollar bills in the right pants pocket and five, tens, and twenties in the left. Most times, they aren't folded, just stuffed in.

That Sunday is the most unique and lucrative Max has ever encountered. Dolores reaches deep into her background, temporarily setting aside her concern and fear for her husband Maury, and sells a boatload of produce. The customers love her, especially since she had a husband fighting the "commies." Minnie schmoozes the older women, and Archie does what he is told with a world-class smile and a positive attitude. Even Shia rises to the occasion and works his ass off.

Business is so good that Max takes the money out of his pockets several times to make room for more. He stuffs the bills, again and again, in paper bags and places them in an opening in the pushcart. A big mistake.

# # #

Usually, the pushcart people close up around one or two o'clock on a Sunday, roughly when the garbage trucks—or "sanitation" people—show up. In recognition of the fees paid to the city for an "Open Air Market License," the city sends out trucks to remove the debris—carrot tops, rotten fruit, spoiled vegetable, and the like—to try and keep the rats at bay.

But this particular Sunday, the closing is not until three or four. By four, the Shpire family is exhausted. Minnie, Dolores, and Archie go home around the corner, and Shia and Max are left to close up.

Suddenly, Max realizes he has put two bags with crumpled money in the pushcart. As he searches desperately for the bags and can't find them, he asks Shia if he has seen them and, if so, where they are. Shia doesn't know but sheepishly suggests that "uh, maybe, uh, the bags were thrown out." It is a significant blow to Max. No one is to blame—it could have been Minnie or Dolores, but what the fuck happened to the money? The garbage trucks have left.

Max runs up the street to the sanitation department supervisor and explains that they have thrown out a bag or two of money. Oddly enough, the supervisor is sympathetic. "Okay, Max, the trucks have left, but they are going to the dumps on Flatlands Avenue, near Canarsie. Get over there as soon as you can, and you might be able to get them. Good luck."

Max turns to Shia and says, "Forget about closing up. We need to head to the city dump, and hundreds of dollars are at stake." And off they go.

# # #

In those days, The City of New York is concerned about landfills and turning swamps into housing areas. The more they can fill the land, the better. The garbage from Blake Avenue is most welcome.

Max and Shia arrive at the dump. They are late, and the trucks from Blake Avenue have already deposited their load. Max, undeterred, marches into the supervisor's office and explains the situation. At first, he couldn't give a shit, but a $20 bill quickly changes his mind. The supervisor shows them where Blake Avenue's garbage is and wishes them good luck scouring through the debris. Max avoids the temptation to throttle him and tells Shia to follow him into the dump.

They follow the directions to the most recent pile of crap. They look over the area repeatedly but can't tell one pile from another. The smell is overpowering, and Shia begins to feel sick. Suddenly, Max recognizes a few of the items he had tossed out. "This is the spot," he says to Shia.

As they start to run through the garbage, two enormous Doberman Pincers appear out of nowhere—junkyard dogs. Barking and growling, they surround Shia, who is in a state of panic. Max, unafraid, says, "Shia stand still. Don't move a muscle. Look away and calmly say nice dogs. Do you have anything on you that you might give them as a treat?" Shia's shaky answer: "Just some nuts."

"Offer it to them...but carefully."

The dogs sniff his hands, seem pleased by the offering, and slowly move on.

The problem is that they need a shovel to dig for the lost money bags. So, they get on their hands and knees and begin to explore, looking for a needle in a garbage pile. Fortunately, Shia saves the day. He notices some lettuce leaves with two bags in their midst. "I got it, Pop," he yells. Max runs over and hugs him. Shia is shocked and can't remember the last time his dad hugged him.

The bags contain seven hundred dollars, an enormous sum in that day. The problem is getting back to the pushcart, stowing it away, and explaining why they were so late to Minnie. One other problem? Their clothes smell of garbage and are soiled and stinking.

Max is too ecstatic and weary to care. Instead of the hamper with the dirty clothes, destined for Archie to bring to the launderette, Max sticks them in Shia and Archie's bedroom closet. When asked later by the kids why he did that, Max says he didn't think Minnie would find out. Seriously? they reply—the whole building stank.

Minnie makes the discovery a day or two later and has a shitfit.

And that's how Minnie got her fur coat. An imitation. But it looked good.

CHAPTER SEVEN
Stay Away from Phoebe

Richie was not happy being back in the office, and neither was his boss, Tom. Working at home during the pandemic fit Richie's lifestyle. No commuting, a new definition of casual dress—his underwear and a clean shirt were all necessary for the Zoom meetings—and best of all, he could nap whenever he wanted to. During the sessions, he could play Wordle while on the call, and no one knew. Of course, there was the time he used his mobile phone and thought he shut off the video and speaker, went to the bathroom during a meeting, and created a new level of sound effects that no one would ever let him forget.

At thirty-two, Richie Beretta was a bit overweight and not very handsome. He more than made up for what he lacked in looks with a sense of humor and his version of charm. He saw himself as a "ladies' man" and got many dates. Women found his curly black hair and hazel eyes attractive.

His boss at the social media company was Tom Simpson, a forty-year-old rising star who runs the company's advertising department. Tall, blond, ruggedly handsome, with charm and guile, Tom was a man's man and a take-no-prisoners type. He was not as sorry to be back in the office as Richie because he loved the casual corridor encounters with his team and was willing to trade off the pleasures of working at home for a return to normal.

Things had gradually returned to a semblance of pre-pandemic normality, but many employees had opted to find other work to continue their at-home work life.

About three months after the mandated return to the office, Richie was at his desk, and Tom walked in.

"So, how's it going?" asked Tom.

"Good, closed a big campaign with Verizon. Mucho dinero."

"Excellent," replied Tom.

"So, when's the hot shot getting here?"

"He's here…and referring to him as a hot shot is the wrong attitude."

"Come on, Tom…I have friends in the LA office, and they couldn't wait to see him go. The guy is a world-class suck-up and not very trustworthy."

"Look," says Tom. "HR told me he's on a fast track, and moving to New York headquarters is part of his training and development. You'll never know where he ends up, so let's not be too rough on him."

"Sure, sure. Another hotshot from La-La land…Want to know something else? He thinks he's god's gift to women. Always coming on to the best-looking or the one who can help him move ahead."

"Give me a break," replied Tom. "As long as I'm your boss, you'll keep your thoughts and mouth shut. We all need to work together. Besides, we lost too many people, and an experienced new person is what we need. Capeesh?"

"What if he goes after Phoebe?"

"Enough! Let it go. He won't."

There was a brief knock on the door, and without waiting for an answer, Mike Bell walked in.

"Hi, am I interrupting?"

Mike Bell was a poster child for California dudes. Tall, blond hair, blue eyes, fit, trim, and looked like he just got off a day at the beach surfing. He sauntered in with a swagger and a twinkle in his eyes. Richie instantly disliked him, and even Tom seemed to have second thoughts. But kept it to himself.

"No, no, it's okay," said Tom. "Come in, Mike…Richie, this is the new guy from LA I was telling you about."

Richie got up and shook hands with Mike.

"Hey Mike, welcome to the Big Apple…from LA, huh? You are not going to like New York City winters."

Mike said, "Nice to meet you, Richie. I'm used to the East Coast weather and like the changing seasons. The weather can be boring in LA. You get up in the morning and look out the window and say, 'Oh, another beautiful, sunny day—wish it would rain for a change.'"

"Really?" said Richie. "And how do you like earthquakes?"

Tom interrupted, "Richie, we need to let Mike know what's what, fill out the paperwork, and tell him what he needs to know."

"Gotcha," replied Richie with an amused look on his face.

"Please handle it. I have a meeting with the IT folks. Call me if you need me." He did a sort of faux salute on his way out the door.

"So, Richie, is that my desk?"

"Yeah."

"Are you sure? Kind of seen better days. And what's with the chair? Have you guys heard about ergonomic chairs? Oh, whatever. What do I need to know?" He was smirking.

"I've been here five years, and there are some simple rules that will make things happen for you."

Mike raised an eyebrow and said, "Rules? Same company, different office. What rules do you have here that are different from LA?"

"You're in the head office. These rules are partly company policy and how we do things around here."

"Such as?"

"Rule number one: don't volunteer for anything because whatever it is, it sucks."

Mike looked surprised. "I'm not sure I buy that. I'm here because I volunteered to lead a task force and committee. It's the route to the fast track, Richie. You might want to think about it."

Richie stared at him momentarily, looking annoyed, but decided to move on.

"Number two. Suck up as much as you can without losing your dignity...if you want to get ahead."

"Now that makes sense. But I prefer to call it 'managing upward' instead of sucking up. That's how you get to the executive floor, dude."

Richie glared at him and said, "Really? And don't call me dude. We may be on an island, but there are no waves here."

"Okay, okay…anything else?"

"Don't shit where you eat…meaning don't date co-workers."

Mike expressed surprise. "How come? That's a ridiculous rule."

Happy to see Mike agitated, Richie replied, "Here at the head office, the company frowns—as in 'you're fired'—if you mess with a co-worker. In other words, keep your dick in your pants when it comes to the people who work here: women, men, or both."

"Aw, come on, out in LA, a bunch of us would go out after work for drinks, and a hook-up or two was known to happen. No one had a problem with it." Mike leaned forward and whispered, "Some of my most memorable nights violated that rule." Then winked at Richie, who replied through clenched teeth, "This is New York. We don't do that here."

"Wait a minute," said Mike. "The guys I worked with in LA said there's a woman here I should get to know. Are you telling me I can't look her up or date her? She is supposed to be amazing—beautiful, sensuous, smart, great figure, terrific in bed—the whole package. Everyone said that getting to know Phoebe is worth the transfer."

Richie was stunned and taken aback. "Did you say 'Phoebe'?"

"Yeah. Who is she, and how do I meet her? I was hoping…"

Richie interrupted him and, almost shouting, said, "Stop!! Remember the don't shit where you eat rule? It's also meant to say, stay away from Phoebe!

"What are you talking about? Rules are meant to be broken, especially that one. Why can't I at least meet her?"

Richie replies in a low emphatic voice, "Listen carefully, man… she will turn on you…you will want to date her and get to know her. You'll want to sleep with her. She might even feel the same way. But do whatever it takes to avoid her. Do you hear me? Do yourself a favor and stay away."

Mike was taken aback. "Whoa, ease up, dude. I hear she is a fine lady. They tell me that not only is she gorgeous but, man o' man, the eyes, the smile, the great sex…I gotta meet her."

Richie raised his voice and said, "Listen to me! She's trouble. Stay the hell away! Holy crap."

Mike smiled. "I hear you. But maybe I'm smitten or just curious: I can't wait to meet her. You guys in New York are just too uptight."

Just then, Tom returned and looked at them. It's clear to him that there have been some disagreements or possibly a full-blown problem.

"What's going on? Why the raised voices?"

Richie breathlessly answered, "First day on the job, and he wants to violate the rule…"

"What rule?" asked Tom. Then, after a moment, the realization set in, and he added, "You don't mean…"

"Yeah, he's getting all worked up about Phoebe." In a whiny tone, "Wants to meet her. Maybe ask her out."

"Oh, sweet Jesus!" Tom said.

Mike stared at them quizzically. "Hey, lighten up, guys. What's the problem?"

"Phoebe! That's the problem," Richie said.

"I understand the rule," said Mike. "I get it. Just saying that I'd like to get to know her."

Both Richie and Tom at the same time shouted, "Forget it!!"

Tom took a deep breath and added, "Mike, Phoebe is an excellent employee, but there are things about her you need to know."

In a condescending and cocky manner, Mike said, "Such as?"

Tom turned to Richie. "We better tell him."

"Everything?"

"Yes, tell him."

Mike was amused, "You guys are too much. What's the big deal?"

Richie had suddenly gotten very serious. A frown crossed his forehead. "Around here, Phoebe is known as the Black Widow. As in black widow spider."

"What the hell are you talking about?" asked Mike.

"You tell him, Tom."

Tom asked Mike, "Do you know what a black widow is?"

"Sure, but what does that have to do with anything?"

Richie jumped in. "I thought this guy was supposed to be smart?"

Tom held his hand in a 'stop' manner and said, "The expression comes from the black widow spider. That's when the female eats the male after mating. Let me put it another way, after they fuck, she kills him."

"What?" Mike said.

Richie chimed in, "Phoebe has a bad history with men. A terrible history."

Mike didn't believe them. "What the hell? You're playing with me. I was told that the way to win her heart is to wine and dine her. I also heard she loves a romantic spot called…"

Tom interrupted. "Listen carefully. Phoebe is beautiful and has that certain look in her eye that men can't resist, like a moth to a flame. More than beautiful, she is charming, smart, and sensuous. But she's toxic."

Mike chuckled. "Get the fuck out of here. Maybe she's worth the risk?"

Richie informed Mike that Phoebe had been a widow many times, and the men she had been with didn't live very long.

All Mike could say was, "Huh?"

"Okay," said Richie. "Consider this. First, one: Phoebe is in college and meets her dream guy. They get engaged. He drops dead on their wedding night in the middle of banging away. Heart attack. Twenty-two years old."

"Doesn't mean a thing," said Mike.

"The guy was a track and field star," replied Richie.

It was Tom's turn, and he added, "Number two. Phoebe dates this married guy, and the relationship is hot and heavy. He leaves his wife to be with Phoebe. They marry. They go on their honeymoon, and he comes home sick. Some bug eats away at his vital organs. A month later, he dies."

Mike was still not impressed or concerned. "Shit happens.

People pick up rare diseases all the time on exotic trips.

"They went to Montreal," says Tom.

"Okay, you're starting to get to me. But I don't want to marry her. I want to meet her."

"Oh yeah?" said Tom. "Let me tell you what comes next." He explained that Phoebe decided it was not a good idea to marry again. She stopped going out but suddenly met someone who fell for her, and she went nuts over him. They start a relationship. No marriage. Just dating."

Mike asked what happened next.

Richie piped up. "Cold, rainy night in late fall, slippery roads, car crashes into a tree and catches on fire. Phoebe gets out easy, but he can't get his seat belt off. By the time the emergency guys get to him, he's toast. By the way, they were on their way to a romantic dinner."

Tom added, "Now she's done with men. Until a year ago."

Mike was getting agitated. "What...What happened?"

Richie said, "She gets her act together and decides to date someone who can care for themselves. She thinks that maybe the jinx is over. She meets and falls in love with a hero cop. They marry."

Tom: "He gets shot on the job. He and his partner answer a call about a man with a gun, and they encounter an 85-year-old man who's bewildered. The old guy pulls out the gun to give it to them, but he farts, and the gun goes off. He's wearing a vest but gets a bullet in the groin and bleeds out...How does that happen?"

Mike was now distraught. "Stop! You're killing me."

Tom said, "No matter how enticing, sexy, and wonderful, stay away!"

"Okay, okay!" said Mike.

"Oh," added Richie, "and she's from Massachusetts."

"What does that have to do with it?"

Tom answered, "From just outside of Salem. She's sweet but strange. Gives me the 'willies' sometimes. She only wears black or red. Sometimes both. No other color."

Richie said, "Tell him about the UPS guy."

Tom asked, "What? Oh, yeah. Which one?"

"Sam," said Richie,

Nervously, Mike asked to know more.

Richie explained, "Sam was our UPS guy for this floor. Hell of a guy. He's delivering packages and bumps into Phoebe. He goes gaga over her and asks her out for a drink that night. The next day at the UPS depot, some guy backs up a truck, knocks him down, and runs over him. Cuts him in half."

"Spooky, huh?" says Tom. "Hey Rich, how about the copy machine repair guy? What was his name? Tony, I think. Yeah, that's it."

"Tony was a flirt," add Richie. "Always coming on to the ladies."

Mike got up and was in the process of freaking out. "I got it. I got it! This is too much! I'll stay away. I need to go to the bathroom." He walked out of the room in a hurry.

Richie looked at Tom and asked, "Think he bought it?"

"Oh yeah."

"The nerve of that guy," said Richie. "Comes here from LA, thinks he's a hot shot and wants to make a move on Phoebe. As if we don't have enough competition."

"What I don't understand," says Tom, "is how they know about her in LA."

"Word travels fast in this company."

"It's amazing. For a computer geek, she sure knows how to party."

Richie remarked, "Just about wore me out last time we were together."

"Yeah," said Tom. "She's tough to keep up with."

"Whose turn is it?" asked Richie.

"Doesn't matter. It's my turn."

"You sure?" said Richie doubtfully.

"Try to remember that I'm your boss."

CHAPTER EIGHT
The Football Nightmare

Maury has what Harvey desperately craves—a season's ticket to the football NY Giants.

Maury is 42, built like a tackle (which he was in high school), a Korean War veteran, and happens to be married to Harvey's sister. Maury tends to be a bit boastful but is a warm and friendly guy overall.

Harvey is somewhat younger at 27, and his sister, Dorsey, is 15 years older than him. She practically raised him, and he spent lots of time at their home, babysitting, watching TV, and just hanging out. What drives him crazy is that on most Sundays in the fall, Maury and twelve of his friends would drive or subway up to The Bronx—Yankee Stadium to be exact—to watch the Giants play football. They all have season tickets.

Harvey can't even watch the home games on TV because, in their greed, the National Football League blocks those games to induce fans to buy tickets. But there are no tickets. All games are sold out. Harvey is frustrated and angry every Sunday when the Giants play at home.

His wife, Maureen, tries to take his mind off things by getting Sunday matinee seats to top Broadway shows. Sometimes that works; mainly, it doesn't help. A few times, she suggests that, since they are trying to have a baby, perhaps Sunday afternoons might be lucky for them. To which Harvey replies rudely, "You're Irish Catholic. Sunday may be fortunate to you but not to this Jew." He sleeps on the couch for most of that week.

They are a handsome couple. At six feet tall, young-looking, and a rising star at a marketing research company, Harvey tends to brood. Maureen is gorgeous, on the short side (which she refers to as "under tall"), but with a sensational figure and great personality, not to mention patience with Harvey. When he frets, she always reminds him that brooding is an Irish tradition, not a Jewish one. That sometimes helps.

One particular Sunday in 1970, Harvey is beside himself because a critical game is only available on the radio, which he hates. Finally, Maureen has had enough. "Will you please talk to Maury and see if you can get one of the season tickets? Maybe someone is moving or can't go to the games, and you could get their ticket."

"Honey," replied Harvey, "These guys have their tickets in their will and leave them to a friend or relative. What's the point?"

But Maureen hates to see him suffer this way and speaks to his sister about it. In addition, Harvey keeps inquiring about the health of the other attendees, such as, "How is Joe feeling after his operation... Has Sam decided to go skydiving? He might like it...I heard Mike fell, did he break a hip..." and so on.

Finally, Maury gets the message. "I'll keep my ears open. These are all great seats."

Then in the summer of 1971, Maury calls Harvey and says, "Hey champ, poor John passed away last week, and his ticket is available. You want it?" In a New York minute, Harvey replies, "Does a bear shit in the woods? Of course, I want the ticket."

"Just one thing you should know. John did not have a seat near most of us. He was a few sections over, not that great, but okay. But if you want it, it's yours." Harvey's answer: "I don't care. I'll take it."

Harvey comes to resent those words.

# # #

The 1971 NFL season is the 52nd regular season of the National Football League. After moving to their new stadium in Foxborough, Massachusetts, the Boston Patriots have changed their name to New England Patriots to widen their appeal to the entire New England region. Harvey is thrilled to be going to the games.

Both families have moved to central New Jersey, and Harvey offers to drive to the games. It starts as a fun outing, but things soon go sideways for Harvey.

His seat is behind the endzone, on an angle that cuts the view of the field diagonally in half. Worse, Yankee Stadium, built in 1923, has steel beams and exposed girders all over that blocked many views. Harvey's seat is two rows behind a beam, a nightmare. It seems to him that every important play took place behind that beam, which cut the field in half and blocked his view. At the first game of the season (and every subsequent game), if Harvey moves to the left to see the action, the person to his right or left did the same, and a collision, accompanied by "watch it!" is the result. He is a wreck after the season opener.

On their way home, Harvey is sullen and quiet. Maury asks him how he likes his seat. "No offense, Maury," says Harvey, "but that seat truly sucks. I now know how John died. He could no longer take it, and the thought of going to the Giant games caused him to croak." Maury just laughs.

The season goes on, and Harvey grows more morose, occasionally lighting a joint, which he believes might help him cope, before each game. It never does.

That year it is announced that the Giants will move to the Meadowlands in New Jersey in three years, playing temporarily at various stadiums in the New York metropolitan area until it is built. Harvey is now thrilled that he no longer has to face the challenge of Yankee Stadium and learns to enjoy football on TV. Maury and his friends are kept on the season's ticket holder list, but Harvey gives his up.

# # #

In 1976, in the Hackensack Meadowlands (often referred to as a swamp), Giants Stadium is built in the Meadowlands Sports Complex in New Jersey. The team has a permanent home at last, in a new, no visible beams or girders, modern, open, and enormous stadium. So, what if it is widely believed that Jimmy Hoffa is buried under one of the end zones? Not my problem, thinks Harvey. The New York Giants playing in New Jersey doesn't faze anyone.

Maury and his fellow ticket holders are given the opportunity to buy season tickets, but not in a block; they are spread all over the stadium. Maury has the chance to buy two seats next to each other, which he does, in case his son, or Harvey, or business clients wants to use them.

Harvey is not the least put out when he learns of this arrangement. The NFL has changed its policy about televising home games and going to an occasional live game is better than making a season commitment. Besides, Maury keeps bragging about how great his new Giant seats are, and the more he does so, the more Harvey becomes skeptical.

Maury invites Harvey to go to the second home game, and, despite his reservations, he jumps at the opportunity.

Harvey drives them both from central New Jersey to the Meadowlands. When they get there, he is shocked at the size of the parking lot. The new stadium has 80,000 seats, almost twice that of Yankee Stadium, and no subway to accommodate fans. Everyone drives. The second surprise is that the "tailgaters" arrive early, all parked close to the entrance. Harvey can only find space at what feels to him a mile away. Whatever. They hike to the gate and make it well before kickoff.

Giants Stadium is enormous. Harvey just gawks at the size and number of seats. He immediately asks Maury, "Where are your seats?"

Maury answers, "They're great," he smiles. "You'll be surprised."

Harvey is surprised, all right. They begin to climb the steps for what feels like forever. The steps are steep, and Harvey is not a fan of heights, much less climbing, moving around people blocking the access, the confinement of it all, an endless hike.

They make it at last. The very last row in the stadium, and to make matters worse, it is behind the endzone. Great, thinks Harvey, I can make this okay if I have three things: gauze for my nosebleed, oxygen to recuperate from the climb and thin air, and a good pair of binoculars to see the action at the other end of the field.

Maury is as proud as could be, "Aren't these seats great?" he keeps saying. Harvey seriously thinks about jumping off the wall behind their last-row seats or pushing Maury off. But the game is good, and Harvey calms down and enjoys it.

That is until they make their way to the car and leave the stadium.

It is not pleasant to walk a mile to find it, then navigate the car through the parking aisles in bumper-to-bumper traffic on the way to the exit. It takes half an hour to exit the stadium. But there is also another unpleasantry.

Maury is not a good driver. No, make that he is someone who is most uncomfortable behind the wheel. Dorsey has a license, but she, too, saw driving as a necessary evil. Harvey and Maureen ride with them on a few occasions—nerve-wracking experiences all-around—and describe them as "tandem" drivers—perhaps a more appropriate description would be "tag team."

It goes something like this.

"Maury, this lane is crowded, move to the outside lane."

"Okay, can I move over now?"

"Not yet, wait."

"Now?"

"Okay… No, there's a car coming."

"Tell me when I can move over?"

"Stay where you are, we'll change lanes soon."

"Wait, slow down!"

"Speed up, now."

Maury's driving makes the ride worse—one foot on the gas and, at the same time, another foot on the brake. Go, stop, go, stop.

Anyone who is a passenger with them is guaranteed to get seasick.

Maury lapses into his routine as Harvey is driving to exit the parking lot. "Turn right… no, stay where you are… wait, it's open on the left, change lanes… never mind, go straight, no, wait, go right…."

It is the longest half hour of Harvey's life. Between the mile-long hike to their seats, the lack of oxygen up there, and the joy of Maury's backseat driving, Harvey comes home a physical and emotional wreck.

"How was the game?' asks Maureen when he gets home. The look on Harvey's face is all the answer she needs.

"The seats sucked. Maury's constant 'aren't these seats good?' drove me crazy. But not as much as the backseat driving as we left the stadium. From what little I could see, it was a good game."

"Are you going again?" she asked.

"We'll see. I'm not going to ask, but if he offers, I might accept."

"Really? You must be nuts. Football by itself is a ridiculous sport: grown men who look like Neanderthals playing with their balls are bad enough. Dealing with Maury is an added touch of insanity. Forget it and say no if he asks. Watch the silly game at home."

"You're right, but the fuss and pestering for tickets over the years kind of makes me feel obligated to accept."

# # #

A few months later, in early December, the Giants have a good shot at making the playoffs, and fans are excited by this rare event. Maury calls and says he has invited a client to go to the game, but he has other plans. Would Harvey want to go? He immediately says yes.

"Just one thing," says Maury. "Last time you went was in September, and it's much colder now, so dress warm and bring a thermos of something hot."

Harvey hears a voice in his head that says, Don't do it, which he ignores.

As the game day draws near, the voice gets louder, and Harvey starts to have second thoughts. A conflict: Does he pass on what might be the game of the year, or does he go and put up with the seats and Maury?

A solution presents itself. He takes a joint with him, hoping it might help him relax and deal with whatever is to come.

The problem is where and when to smoke it. He can't raise the subject with Maury, who is to the right of Genghis Khan and paranoidly convinced of what he thinks of liberal weed smokers. Let's put it this way: for him, George Wallace was too liberal.

As luck would have it, they stop at a deli to pick up some

sandwiches, which Maury goes in to buy. Harvey takes the opportunity to fire up his 'doobie.'

They get to the stadium, park a mile away, and trek to the seats. Man, it is cold. "Glad I put on long johns," says Harvey through chattering teeth. "Don't worry," replies Maury. "Great game, great seats, you won't feel the cold." "Hmm," mutters Harvey. But what he wants to say is Bullshit! But holds his tongue.

They climb the Mt. Everest of stadiums, with sandwiches and thermoses full of coffee, wearing heavy coats, with Harvey thinking about the Bataan Death March. "Dear God," thinks Harvey, "what the hell am I doing?"

They arrive at their last row of stadium seats. The short wall behind them is not nearly enough to block the cold and wind. The artic gear they are wearing is, well, worthless. The cold goes through their bones, and Harvey is shivering. Maury is fine, in his element, raving about the seats and predicting a great game. Thoughts of throwing Maury over the wall continue to swirl around Harvey until he realizes that this is indeed a great game. He gets into it.

In the second quarter, Harvey's elation begins to wane. The cold and half a thermos of coffee have begun to affect his bladder. Several conflicts accompany this 'aw shit' moment. First, if I ignore it, I won't need to go. Turns out that is just wrong. Second, he thinks, maybe I can hold off until halftime? What, and by the time I get there, so will half the stadium, and I'll be waiting forever to get a urinal. Can I turn around and use the wall behind us? Gross and embarrassing. And on and on, thinking about options, finding no solution, and not concentrating on the game at all.

Harvey decides to bite the bullet, so to speak, mutters something to Maury, and begins the march down the stadium to the men's room. Lots of other fans have had the same idea, and the stairs are crowded. Now, Harvey is in a panic and sweating despite the freezing cold. He's worried that he will be most embarrassed if he doesn't get there soon, and his coat is not long enough to hide the evidence.

Providence decides to smile at Harvey and, with legs almost crossed and a duck walk, he manages to make the bathroom just as someone is leaving a urinal.

Relieved, mentally, and physically, Harvey's good fortune is short-lived. It is now halftime, and the entire stadium is heading down to the men's room. Getting back to his seat is like swimming upstream.

When the second half starts, Harvey is quiet and sullen and can't wait to go home.

# # #

Maury invites Harvey to a game the following football season, which he politely refuses. He has had it with going to live games. The call of nature, among other things, can be accomplished by stopping the broadcast, taping it, and resuming after taking care of things. And it's warm, the food and drink are abundant and easily accessible, not to mention the comfort of an easy chair.

At midseason, a work colleague of Harvey's tells him he has four tickets to a NY Giants-NY Jets game, a rare interleague event, and would like to bring a friend. Harvey's immediate reaction is, No frigging way. But before turning his friend down, he adds, "Oh, and the seats are in the lower mezzanine on the forty-yard line. Behind the Giant's bench." Harvey is struck speechless. "There're from Sports Illustrated, so you know they are good and come with VIP parking."

Harvey is elated and tells his friend to count him in and that he is bringing his brother-in-law Maury.

Gameday.

Harvey says nothing about the seats, and Maury realizes that the Meadowlands Stadium currently houses the Giants and the Jets. Since it's considered a Jets home game, Maury's tickets are not usable, and he's happy to go to this game.

They get to their seats with little to no problem. All of them, especially Maury, are in awe of where they are seated. All parts of the field are well visible, and there's an overhang from the sections above, so it's warm and cozy. Bathrooms and food stands are a short walk away.

Harvey looks up and turns to Maury while pointing toward Maury's seats way off in the distance. In an abrupt, staccato voice, he says, "Maury, these are great seats. Up there in the clouds are shit seats. Great seats here…real shit seats up there."

Maury smiles wanly.

CHAPTER NINE
The Co-op Interview

If one can afford it, owning a home in NYC is better than renting a place to live. In the outer boroughs like Brooklyn or Queens, home ownership is a house, sometimes attached to others, sometimes freestanding; some are one-family, others multi-family units. It varies from neighborhood to neighborhood.

In Manhattan, on the other hand, home ownership mainly involves an apartment in an upscale neighborhood. But now, the choice is whether to buy a condominium or a cooperative (co-op) apartment. Both involve ownership, but a condo has relaxed management and is more flexible. For example, co-ops are notoriously difficult to get into because of a tough board made up of elected homeowners whose screening process can sometimes be draconian. Many condos allow for subletting. Co-ops very rarely do and have the reputation of being friendlier and more community oriented.

For Harvey and Ellen Sharp, condos are less desirable than a co-op. So, when they decide to get a second home in the city, they focus on it.

Harvey is 48, tall and, some would say, handsome, with a pleasant and friendly demeanor but a short fuse for a temper. He is the Chief Marketing Officer for the 3rd largest spirits and wine company worldwide, in charge of the Americas. As he often puts it, from Canada to Chile. It's a tough family-controlled business with difficult owners, customers, and colleagues. He has survived and flourished because he's tough, street-smart, and doesn't suffer fools.

Ellen is his anchor and keeps him focused. They have known each other since their college days—married right after graduation—and she doesn't put up with his shit. She is a head shorter than him, stunning and funny, always fashionably dressed, and with a smile that could melt an iceberg. What Harvey loves about her is that she speaks her mind and, unlike the other wives at the company, has an amazing sense of self. No airs: what you see and hear is what you get.

They lived in Freehold, NJ, while their kids grow up, but as lifelong New Yorkers yearn to return to the city. In 1993, their dream starts to come true. Harvey's career takes off further, and he spends more and more time in the city with late-night meetings and tons of travel. The kids grow up, graduate college, and leave the nest for good. Ellen is not ready to sell the house and move. Her friends and social life are centered on Freehold, and she wants to stay, at least most of the week. Their short-term solution is to get a place in Manhattan where Harvey can stay during the week. It is often referred to as a pied-à-terre, a term they both hate and think pretentious.

Harvey, despite his crazy schedule, finds time to hunt for a place to live. With his older daughter's help and seeing many apartments, they find one on the Upper East Side with a view of the East River. Truth be told, Harvey would prefer the charm of the west side, but this is most convenient to his office. For a guy who grew up in a three-floor walkup in a poor neighborhood in Brooklyn, falling asleep to the sounds of mice scurrying, this is beyond attaining an aspiration. This is amazing.

A "white glove" building with both a 24-hour doorman and concierge is more than they could hope for. The neighborhood that abuts the river is quiet and residential, with amazing restaurants a short walk away. Harvey wants this more than anything, and fortunately, Ellen agrees.

An offer is made and accepted, the mortgage quickly secured. But something gnaws at Harvey.

They don't use an agent and negotiate directly with the apartment owner. Harvey offers a lower price than asked, to which the owner says, "Listen, I got more than I asked from someone else, but you are more likely to pass the Board than they, so I want to sell to you, but at the asking price. No less." *What the fuck*, thinks Harvey. *They'll take less money to get someone who will pass a board interview? What is this about?*, he wondered.

# # #

It is a hot and humid evening in late August and pouring out, a storm accompanied by thunder and lightning. The office door to the meeting room opens, and Harvey walks in. His raincoat is soaked. He takes it off as soon as he enters, and his suit and shirt are partly wet from the rain and partly wet from the general dampness of the humidity. He sees Ellen and sits down next to her.

Ellen looks at him and says, "I'm glad you got here on time. You're soaking wet."

Harvey replies angrily, "It's really coming down. I'm not just wet from the rain...I rushed to get here...it's fucking steaming out there...then the clouds opened up...I got splashed by a cab...couldn't get one and had to run over here. Of course, I'm wet!"

"Calm down. Here are some tissues to dry off. They're running late, so you have a few minutes."

"This is bullshit," is his reply.

"Keep your voice down."

"No, really…"

Just then, a man dressed in work clothes enters the reception area from the conference room. "Hi. Youse must be the Sharps. Nice to meetcha." They shake hands.

"I'm Harvey and this is my wife Ellen," mutters Harvey.

"I'm Norb. Norbert Bryant. But everyone calls me Norb. I'm the super at Giles House." He lets out a nervous laugh. "Actually, I'm the guy who runs the place. Whatever youse need, ask Norb… That's if you pass."

Just then, there's a shout from the meeting room. Sheldon Weiner, the board president, calls out, "Norb! Come back here."

"Whoops. Gotta go. Just came out to tell ya that it'll be another 10 or 15 minutes. They got some business to discuss first."

Ellen replies, "Thanks, we're okay," as Norb slinks off.

In a stage whisper, Harvey, beside himself with exasperation, tells Ellen he thinks this is total nonsense. Ellen replies, "You're the one who wants to live in the city. You're the one who found the Giles House. So, let's go with it, okay? Did you get them the information?"

"Yeah, yeah. I figured that with all the shit they were asking from us, I might as well have Mary put it together. So, she put it in loose-leaf folders and organized it. Took her the better part of a day."

"So, it'll be impressive."

"I don't know who these assholes think they are. There is nothing about our lives that these total strangers don't know by now."

"Well, it's a co-op, and they want to know who is buying. They want to approve the buyers. Makes sense."

"Ellen," says Harvey, "They know more than they need to know."

"Stop it. You wanted a co-op in the city. That's what they do. Condos don't have this kind of interview process."

"Come on...we put a lot of money down, got easily approved for a mortgage, so what else do they need?" Ellen's answer is that all co-ops make you go through this.

"Really? They have our tax returns for the past three years. They have a statement of net worth. They have references from friends, coworkers, and my boss—I really enjoyed asking him for that so he could sneer at me and give me some shit about being able to afford a second home...They have a ten-page questionnaire covering everything about us, including whether we prefer our toilet paper to be dispensed from the top or from the bottom of the roll. I even gave them a reference from Father Robert."

"Stop," says Ellen. "This is the last step. Just deal with it and stop griping."

"You know what really pisses me off? They have enough information to decide, but we must appear in person. Want to know why?"

"Not really," replies Ellen. "but I'm sure you'll tell me."

"To see if we look like we belong…Make sure that neither of us is transsexual or gay…Make sure we don't dress or act weird…But what they really want to know—the real reason we're here—is whether we're people of color."

Ellen is shocked. "What are you talking about? Not many black people are named Harvey and Ellen Sharp."

"What? Maybe they want to be sure we didn't change it from Sharpton."

"You're being ridiculous."

"Have you ever seen a black person in the building all the times we went there?"

"Have you ever met or heard of a black person named Harvey?"

"Yeah, but you could be a black person or, heaven forbid, a Latina…Gotta keep Giles House pure…So, we have to sit here sweating like pigs to appear before the exalted Board."

"Stop working yourself up."

"My whole life bared naked in front of a group of strangers plus the indignity of an inquisition, and you want me to be cool with it?"

"Lower your voice," snaps Ellen.

Norb comes out of the conference room and approaches the Sharps. He tells them that the Board is ready to see them. From the look on his face, he has more than that in mind.

"Just one thing, first," says Norb. "I kinda primed the pump for youse, so to speak. I told them what a nice couple youse are and let 'em know that you'd be a welcome addition to the Giles House."

Harvey looks at him and says, "What? You don't even…"

Ellen interrupts and says, "That's very nice of you Norb. Thanks. Uh, Mr. Sharp and I need a moment. We'll be right in."

As Norb leaves them, Harvey turns to Ellen and is livid. "Did you hear that? We're not even in the friggin' building yet, and he's shaking us down. I guess Christmas is coming…"

"Okay. That's enough. You want a place in the city for the work week. It's a great apartment with a terrific view. But I'm perfectly happy in Freehold. We don't have to do this. So, yes, or no… Will you shut up and suck it up, or do we go home right now? I mean it!"

"But Ellen…," says Harvey sheepishly.

"You want to commute three hours a day."

"On a good day," he replies.

"Exactly my point. Now deal with these people the way you deal with your customers or the shitheads in the company."

Harvey nods his head in agreement. Once again, Ellen has set him straight, and he appreciates it. They enter the conference room, and the seven board members, Norb, and the management agent are at the table. They warmly smile and greet Ellen and Harvey, talk about the humid weather, and introduce themselves. There is Sarah Murphy, the managing agent, gruff on the outside, but they can tell she's smart and caring. Sheldon Weiner is the President, an older man and sharp as a razor. Harvey senses that, like himself, he doesn't suffer fools.

The treasurer is warm and friendly, and very smart. She seems to be the most competent. But the rest are peculiar. The pompous physician, the very ignorant woman who can't seem to put two words together, the attention deficit millionaire who is dressed like a fool, a pompous ambulance chaser lawyer—in other words, a motley crew.

Despite his success and accomplishments, Harvey is still that kid from Brooklyn who grew up poor. He never judges people and always gives the benefit of the doubt. But somehow, this 'circus' is beyond his patience. Ellen, sensing as much, squeezes his hand under the table. He turns to her with a look that says, Don't worry, I can do this. Ellen is not so sure—she is on guard.

Sheldon welcomes them to the meeting, says a few words about the building, and they begin the interview.

Sarah starts. "Will you be harboring a dog?"

Harvey answers, "I don't understand. We have a dog. We don't harbor her. She is part of the family and…"

Ellen quickly interrupts, "Yes, her name is Lucy, and she's a cute little Havanese."

The pompous lawyer chimes in. "I hate dogs. Sheldon, how many times do I have to tell you we should become a dog-restricted building, not dog-friendly." In a nasty voice, he goes on, "How much does it weigh? How tall is it? Does it bite?"

Harvey is about to jump over the table, grab this asshole by the throat, and beat the shit out of him. As he starts to get up, Ellen pulls him back and answers. "She's a small dog, around 15 pounds, and at that weight, she obviously can't be very tall."

Harvey jumps in, "On the other hand, she could be a very

large, very skinny dog. Or a malnourished pony."

"Tell me, Fred…is it?" he goes on. "Have you ever seen the Peter Sellers movie where he has a dog on a leash and asks if his dog bites? He says no. The dog then bites someone, who says you told me your dog doesn't bite. To which the Sellers character says, 'It's not my dog.'"

Only one or two people laugh.

Ellen jumps in, "My husband is such a kidder."

Sarah pipes up. "Are you aware of the Giles House rules about cleaning up after your dog, using the service elevator only, not going through the lobby, and not barking?"

"What about biting?" asks Harvey.

Ellen jumps in. "Shush, Harvey. My husband likes to kid around. Now's not the time for your joking, dear." Turning to Sarah, she adds, "Yes, we have read the house rules and know all the dog-related requirements."

The pompous doctor takes his head out of his phone and asks, "Do you entertain much?"

Sheldon interrupts him. "Please hold off, doc. Let me ask some questions."

"So, Mr. and Mrs. Sharp…may I call you Harvey and Ellen?" They answer, yes, of course.

"We've gone over your papers and documents, and I must tell you that this is the best presentation we've ever seen. Very professional. No one has ever organized it into books before. We're impressed. And I should also tell you that we all saw it in advance and are comfortable with sufficient information. Isn't that, right?" The Board all nod except Fred, the lawyer. "Just one question. Sharp, your family name. Was it always Sharp, or was it changed?"

Harvey jumps in and says, "Yes, it used to be Sharpton. Do you know my cousin Al? He ran for President and has been active and vocal in NYC politics."

"Stop fooling around, Harvey." To the Board, "Harvey's family name has always been Sharp."

Sheldon replies, "I knew a guy named Sharp, and it used to be Shapiro."

"Ah, and a Shapiro wouldn't make the cut?"

"What?" says Sheldon.

Ellen again jumps in. "Please go on, Mr. Weiner…uh, Sheldon… um, Shelly."

Sheldon asks Harvey about his work. Specifically about his working for a spirits and wine company. Harvey explains that he runs marketing for the Americas.

The doctor jumps in and wants to know if they have loud parties and if they drink a lot. Harvey smiles his faux smile and gently, but sarcastically, says that just because he is in the alcohol industry doesn't mean he's a boozer if that's what the doctor is getting at. He adds that if a doctor is a urologist, does that make him a prick?

A hush falls over the room.

Sheldon breaks the silence and changes subjects. "Harvey, we have a Holiday party every year. Could you supply the wine and save the co-op some money? Just a case or two."

Harvey answers that he can't do that, at which point Ellen punches him in the thigh.

He goes on, "I'd like to help, but the laws in New York prevent me from giving wine away. Sorry. I can't. But I'll ask the attorneys."

Sheldon indicates he understands. Harvey then asks if they can move on and if they are accepted into the building.

Sheldon asks them to wait outside for a few minutes. They leave.

Harvey is beside himself and says to Ellen, "What the fuck? Is this the 5th grade, and we need to step out to see who's the class president?" Ellen shrugs.

After a few minutes, they are called back in.

Sheldon says, "We're happy to have you as neighbors. As I said, just looking at your documents, we had already made up our minds. Welcome to Giles House. Congratulations."

They all stand and extend their hands in congratulations.

Harvey won't let it go. "I guess you just wanted to see us in person. I mean what we looked like."

Ellen glares at him. She starts to get up and leave, but Harvey remains seated. "Just a minute, please. I want to clarify a few things." They sit down.

Harvey says, "If I may, before we close on the apartment, now that we have your okay to buy, I have a few questions."

Ellen stares at him in astonishment.

Sheldon smiles and says, "Sure. What do you want to know?"

"The pre-war buildings across the street, the whole block, are only six stories. The apartment we want is on the 11th floor. What if those buildings are razed, and a high rise goes up? We will lose our view of the river, and the value will come down."

Sheldon tells him that cannot happen because the buildings are landmarked and can't be torn down. Harvey is a bit skeptical and asks if they would mind if Sarah would be so kind as to send some documentation of the landmark status. Sheldon is quick to agree and asks her to take care of it. "Anything else?" he asks Harvey.

Harvey smiles inwardly and is now into what he feels is payback. "Well. Shelly, you and the Board know a great deal about me—actually, all there is to know—but I don't know anything about you. And after all, we'll be neighbors."

"What do you mean?"

"Well, for example, what do you do for a living? What references do you have? Can I see a letter from your priest of rabbi…?

Ellen holds up her hand in front of Harvey's face in a 'stop' manner. She turns to Sheldon and says, "I told you Harvey was a kidder. You'll love his sense of humor when you get to know him." Then to Harvey, she adds, "That's enough, dear. These folks have other business to attend to, and we should…"

Harvey says, "Yeah, okay. But, really, Sheldon, what do you do?"

Sheldon is a bit flustered, but he answers that he owns a real estate brokerage in Queens. Harvey continues his interrogation and asks how long he's been the co-op president, how many children he has, their ages, and so on. Next, he goes to the other board members and tries to continue grilling until Ellen jumps in. "Harvey, we need to go. We're having dinner with Jimmy and Karen and will be late."

Harvey gives in but takes one more shot as they get up to leave: "I guess we need to go. Thanks for your time. We're delighted to be part of the Giles House. But a small favor, please..."

Sheldon asks him to go on.

"Those books with my finances and life story in them... I'd like them back. You don't need them anymore, and I'm sure you can appreciate that I don't want all that personal information lying around."

Sheldon indicates that he understands and will have Sarah return them.

Harvey and Ellen, at last, stand up and are ready to leave. "Thanks again," says Harvey. Have a good night."

While waiting for the elevator, Ellen turns to Harvey and says, "You're an asshole. Remind me to stop at Walgreens on the way home to get you some Preparation H. You could have blown the whole thing."

"Yeah," replies Harvey, "but we got in. Told you all they cared about was our skin color. It was all a sham."

"Oh, and since when is there a restriction on giving wine for parties? How many cases from your unlimited allotment for Melissa's wedding did you get? And what about all the booze you gave for the church bazaar?"

"That's different," says Harvey. "My policy is no free booze for shitheads."

"Very cute. Let's go."

"While we are on that topic," asks Harvey, "when did our Lab, our over 50-pound Lab, become a small, cute Havanese?"

"Seemed like the thing to say at the time," answers Ellen.

"What are you going to do when they find out?"

"I'll deal with it," replies Ellen. "I think you'll be running for the Board soon, and when you get elected, you'll change the policy."

CHAPTER TEN
Prison Food

Marvin Rosen is a 38-year-old investment banker serving 3 to 5 years at the Federal Correctional Institute in Otisville, NY. Fortunately, he is in the minimum-security area known as the camp. Up the hill is the medium security, where the hardened criminals are stored. Marvin has been convicted of insider trading, and his fellow prisoners are almost all white-collar criminals.

Marvin is five foot eleven, muscular—thanks to the boredom of prison life—with curly brown hair and deep blue eyes. His older brother Irv relentlessly teased him about the blue eyes as they grew up. He used to say, "A Jew with blue eyes and curly brown hair is a Jew whose ancestor slept with a Cossack." Eventually, he stopped saying it as Marvin's success and wealth increased and became enviable.

As a Wall Street type, Marvin is a schemer and always has something up his sleeve. As you might expect, Marvin is used to the good life, and while he can tolerate the confinement to some extent, he can't deal with the food. So, he is always working some grift or con. Sometimes he gets away with it. Most times, he doesn't. But he keeps on trying.

It is the spring of 1990, and Passover is just a month away. Thereby giving Marvin an idea. He asks to see the Warden with an important request, which is granted based on his relationship with the head guard.

\# \# \#

Michael Donovan is the assistant warden at FCI Otisville. He is 55 years old and has been passed up for promotion to warden more times than he can care to recall. A ruddy-cheeked Irishman, Donovan, is very tall, skinny, and with a perpetual scowl. His anger and bitterness are palpable, and after 25 years in the Bureau of Prisons, he hates everyone and everything and is counting the days until he can retire and pursue his passion for deep-sea fishing.

This morning, he is ignoring the beautiful spring day, doing paperwork, and ruminating over the wise guys from New York City who represent a significant portion of the prison population. The kikes and wops, as he refers to the Jews and Italians, are cheaters and liars, he fumes, and the damn courts let them off too easy.

There's a knock on the door, and Donovan shouts 'Enter.' One of his Lieutenants, Vern Negus, walks in with his hand firmly on Marvin Rosen's arm and moves him close to Donovan's desk. Marvin decides to take a seat at a chair in front of the desk. Donovan stares at him incredulously. "Who the fuck told you to sit down," he screams. "And what the fuck do you want? Negus, why do you keep bringing this heeb in to see me? Huh? What's wrong with you?"

Without waiting for an answer, he glares at Marvin and asks him, "What is it this time?"

Marvin comes back with, "What, no, hello, no, how are you, Marvin?"

Donovan throws his pen down, pushes his chair away from the desk, and stands up with clenched fists. "Don't fuck with me. What do you want?"

Marvin calmly tells him he asked to see him to make an official request. To which Donovan shouts, "Another one?" Turning to Negus, "Why do you keep letting him talk you into seeing me?"

Negus' sheepish reply is, "What was I supposed to do? He kept asking and reading the regulations to me."

"Get him a fucking suggestion box."

Marvin starts to interrupt and talk about his prison rights and rules. Donovan tells him to shut up. "I know the rules. This candy-ass minimum-security bullshit allows all of you prima donnas to bust our balls. I wished they'd lock up you money-grubbing... aw, what's the use. What do you want? Let's see, there is not enough TV time? More channels? I know, a heated pool? Maybe more hot water for the shower? Maybe soap on a rope, so you don't have to bend down..." He laughs hysterically at his joke, then stops abruptly.

Marvin replies that more privacy would be nice, to which Donovan shouts at Negus to get him the hell out of here. "Wait a minute, please, Warden," Marvin says.

Donovan says, "Between the embezzlers... the insider traders... and the mobsters who those dumb ass DAs can only get on tax evasion... Christ, I wish I was back with druggies and murderers. This is a friggin' country club! Get to the point and get out."

"Passover is coming up," is Marvin's reply.

"And I give a shit because...? Passover? The Jew...uh, Jewish holiday? So, fucking what?"

Marvin explains that it's an important holiday for Jewish people, and they only eat kosher Passover food. The Warden reminds him that he had the opportunity to eat Kosher food, and he turned it down. Why does he want it now?

"Let me explain," says Marvin. If you keep kosher, there is still stuff you can eat here. But for Passover, it all must be kosher for Passover: no bread, nothing made with grain, that kind of thing."

"Since when are you so religious?" snarls Donovan.

Marvin says, "Since I got here. I mean, being in prison makes you look at life differently."

Donovan sighs and tells Marvin he will bring it up with the prison superintendent and asks what kind of food and for how long.

Marvin explains that it's not for him only but for all the Jewish prisoners who want it. Donovan tells him that he's pushing it. Marvin goes on, "Look, I'll call my brother and have the food shipped in. All you'll have to do is receive it and inspect it. Warden, I checked the prison regulations and…"

"I said I would talk to the boss. Now get the hell outta here."

The guard and Marvin leave. As they are walking away, Marvin thanks Negus and says, "I don't think he has a choice. Unreal, a few weeks without the shit prison food."

Negus seems worried about what just happened and about his career. Marvin assures him not to worry about it. He adds, "Let me have your retirement plan, and I'll go through it. Make sure you fill out the long-term goals and include a budget and current cash need." Negus agrees and says he will leave it on

Marvin's bunk.

# # #

The next day, Marvin is sitting in the prison yard, reading. Ray Lorenzo walks up to him. Ray is 55 years old and looks like he just walked off the set of Goodfellas. Tall, very tan, muscular, and very Mediterranean-looking. It's also obvious that he is not a man to be messed with. He sits down next to Marvin. He's in the joint for tax evasion and is doing 8 to 10.

"You the one they call Mr. Wall Street?"

"I guess," says Marvin.

He asks Marvin if he'd like a smoke. Marvin thanks him but lets him know that cigarettes are not his thing. He prefers to use them as 'currency' and barter. He explains that cigarettes are as good as money on the inside, and not smoking gives him the opportunity to do some trades for what he really wants.

Ray stares at him. "Smart boy. Tell me something...how'd you get caught, a smart guy like you?"

"I got greedy," is Marvin's reply.

They smile at each other and appear to be developing a friendship. Ray asks Marvin what the hell is inside trading, anyhow. He asks if it's like knowing which horse is going to win in a race. Marvin explains that that's right. "What are you in for, tax evasion?" asks Marvin.

"Yeah. The same problem as you... greedy and then my luck ran out. Also, I had some dumb fucks working for me and left a trail that a baby could follow... Which brings me to the purpose of my visit."

Marvin says, "Hold on Ray…uh, Mr. Lorenzo…I…

"Call me Bagels."

"What," says Marvin. "Why bagels?"

"When I was a kid running numbers out of a bagel store, I kept the chits and money in a bag of bagels. Guys liked the idea, 'cept for the time the bag was full of garlic bagels, and the money stank for a week. The boss said it was like marked bills. Nearly got my ass kicked. Ever since then, my nickname's been 'bag o' bagels.'"

Marvin starts to laugh hysterically but catches himself and stops. "It's okay, kid, it is kind of funny," says Ray.

Marvin goes on, "What can I do for you, Ray, ur, Bagels?"

Ray looks around to see if anyone is in earshot, then continues. "Just been thinking that I can use a guy like you. It's difficult when you run a cash business, the money piles up. I need a smart boy like you to help me figure it out. Where to put it, how to pay my taxes, so the Feds don't get wise, that kinda thing. Wanna talk about the details?"

"Bagels, I got busted for insider trading and lost my life, my job, my career. My wife had our second kid, and I won't be around to watch her crawl, babble, or take her first steps. I think my life of crime is over when I get out."

"Who the fuck is talking crime? I need an investor. Someone to find businesses to put money in. Mine and maybe the boys."

Marvin loses his bravado and tells Ray that when he is out, he may go into teaching or some other job that will let him be part of his family without ever serving time again. He gets increasingly nervous and stammers a bit.

Ray stares at him and says, "Relax, kid. This ain't no movie or TV show. Nobody gonna make an offer you can't refuse. But when you get on the outside, you might find some legit business opportunities that need some dough. Maybe we can do business someday. All's I'm sayin'."

Marvin relaxes. But Ray comes back with, "Maybe we can do some business here."

Ray then says that he has received a whole Genoa salami and provolone, and how about trading his stuff for three cartons of cigarettes?

Marvin starts to negotiate and offers two cartons. "What's the matter?" asks Ray. "You don't eat Genoa Salami?" Marvin explains that he eats everything except the putrid prison food.

They go back and forth and settle on Ray's offer. Odd bedfellows have become friends.

# # #

After Ray leaves, Warden Donovan, accompanied by prison guard Negus, walks up to Marvin as he is reading. "Okay, Rosen, your wish has been granted. Turns out the info you gave the US Attorney has led to a bunch of plea bargains, and lots of your insider people are signing and singing like canaries. Want to hear something funny?"

"Sure," says Marvin.

"Two guys in suits knock on the door to the house of a potential witness—at least that's what they thought—one guy from the AG's office and the other FBI. The man opens the door and takes one look at the two Feds, and they see his knees start to shake…Then say, "Hello, are you Mr. So and So?" The man answers with, "Come in, I'll tell you who was involved and how they did it." Didn't ask for ID and didn't wait to hear what they wanted. For all, he knows the guys could have been Jehovah's Witnesses. So, he spills his guts. Unbelievable. Your people are stand-up guys, all right. Ha!"

"Is that what you came to tell me, Warden?"

"Oh yeah…well, your guardian Angel tells the Bureau of Prisons commissioner, who tells the Super, who tells my boss—a long trail of shit flowing downhill here—who tells me to treat you special and let you have the Passover food. So, call who-the-fuck-ever and have it shipped in."

Marvin starts to thank him, but Donovan angrily cuts him off and warns him they will be checking every item and that they better not find contraband.

Marvin's smart-ass reply, "Absolutely. No gunpowder in the matzah balls, knives in the brisket, or gefilte fish grenades. I got it."

Donovan glares at him, "You are a wise ass. If it were up to me, I'd move you up the hill to the rock and see where your big mouth takes you, especially when you get to a room with a biker named Bubba. But you got your friends, so get outta my face and choke on your matzah."

As he walks away, Negus hangs back for a moment. He says, "Thanks for the advice, but are you sure about Apple?" Marvin assures him, and they both leave the area.

# # #

A day or two later, Marvin's wife, Sheila, comes to see him on visitors' day. She is 37, tall, slender, and very attractive.

As a minimum-security prison, there is no partition, but touching is not permitted, and a prison guard stands casually in the background.

Marvin and Sheila make small talk about the kids, family, money matters, and the likelihood of an early release. At last, Sheila asks, "What's this business about Passover food? And, since when did you become religious? You always said that Passover food upsets your stomach."

Marvin explains that he still feels that way, but it beats the junk he has to eat in prison. He has a chance to enjoy something else for a week or two. "Tell Irv to send a week's worth of food for ten people—the Jewish prisoners. Those who don't want it, no problem, I'll use the food to trade."

They continue to talk about the food, then what he will do when he gets out, and the new baby. Time runs out, and Sheila tells him she will talk to Irv, then leaves.

The next day, Marvin is in the exercise area, and Vern Negus comes over to him. "So, what kind of food is your brother sending you?" he asks. "The kind of food we eat on Passover, plus prepared meat, fish, and chicken meals. Just got to heat 'em up," Marvin replies.

Negus says, "Do you know what would be a nice gesture? Do you some good too."

"What?" Asks Marvin.

"Get some food for the guards. The slop they serve us is no

better than what the inmates get."

They continue talking about it, and Negus tells him there are 25 people on his shift. That's all they need. Marvin tells him he will take care of it, walks to the pay phone, and makes a call. It is to his brother Irv.

The conversation goes like this:

"That's collect from Marvin Rosen…Okay, I'll hold…Irv, how are you? Yeah, yeah…That's great…I'm happy to hear that…When are you coming out? Okay, I understand…Listen Irv, did Sheila tell you about the food? That's right, enough for ten for the whole week…But, Irv, it just changed…Listen, and I'll explain…If I had more food, I could take care of the guards…Right…The extras will also be good for trading…No dummy, not that kind of trading. I mean barter…Yeah, for 35 people…take it easy, take it easy…So instead of a van, get a small truck. Go to U-Haul…A small truck… Talk to Sheila. She has the money…I appreciate it, Buddy…Listen, there are people waiting to use the phone. I'll have to call you back another time. Just get the food…Thanks…You too."

Marvin tells Negus that it's all set but warns him about Matzah. "It's unleavened bread, so it's without yeast and more like a cracker than bread. It gives you indigestion going down and clogs you up going out. It's been referred to as the bread of affliction."

"Why?" asks Negus.

Marvin tells him he'll find out if he eats it for a week. He goes on to say that Negus should stick to the prepared meals.

The guard leaves, and Ray walks up to Marvin.

"Mister Wall Street! How's the market? Whatcha up to?"

"Hi, Bagels. How are you?"

"Rumor has it that you and Warden Donovan have become good buddies."

Marvin asks where he had heard that.

"Well, I got my sources. They tell me that—one—youse been in to see him a few times, and he's been known to pay you a visit or two, and—B—he's getting the word from on high to treat you kindly and—tree—you and him got some deal going on. What's the story kid, or should I say boychick?"

"Boychick?"

"Yeah, I learnt that word in the bagel shop, and don't change the subject."

Marvin protests and tells Ray it's not a big deal.

Ray gets annoyed. "No big deal? Just because this is white-collar-crime-ville don't mean a guy can't get hurt in here. There's a code. It's them and us. It's bad enough that youse cooperated with the Feds. No one specs you guys to be stand-up. But in here, the rules are different."

Marvin explains, "Passover is coming up, and I conned the Warden to let me get some Passover food for the Jewish prisoners. That's all—a week's break from the slop.

"Smart move to come clean. That's what I heard. And why, may I ask, did you decide to include the guards?"

Marvin says, "Well, they kind of invited themselves."

"Looks bad to the boys, boychick," says Ray.

Marvin explains it would be good for business if they were included—a goodwill gesture. Ray smiles, agrees with Marvin, and lets him know he will calm everything down. But he has an additional gesture. "Passover time is also Easter time. How about you include me and the boys in the food you're bringing in? Tell you what. You get us Passover food, and when Christmas comes around, and we get to bring in food for the holidays, we include you and your friends. But not the guards."

Seeing no other choice, Marvin shakes Ray's hand and says, "Deal." Ray smiles, nods his head, pinches Marvin's cheek, and walks off. Marvin hurries over to the phone.

"Collect from Marvin Rosen…I'll hold…Irv! Glad I got you. That's what I'm calling about…That's great but…Listen Irv, it's getting more complicated…What do you mean 'what now'…Hey, if you were in here, there's nothing I wouldn't do to help…Fine, Irv, you're right, you're too honest…C'mon, are you going to listen to me or not? Forget about the small truck…Can you get a hold of a tractor-trailer?"

Holding the phone away from his ear, he said, "Stop yelling! Let me explain and tell you what I need…"

# # #

A few weeks later, Marvin is standing in the yard, and Warden Donovan and Guard Negus walk up to him. *Uh-oh*, thinks Marvin.

"Think you're cute, don't ya?"

"What?" asks Marvin.

The Warden is getting angry, and his face turns red. "My

kid comes home from Penn State with his Jewish roommate for spring break. So, I ask his friend about Passover food, and you know what? Ravioli is definitely not kosher for Passover. Neither is Italian wedding soup. Oh, and I don't need the kid to tell me that a baked ham ain't kosher for anything. Not to mention calamari and shrimp. Think I'm a moron?"

Marvin says, "But…"

"But nothing. I come back from vacation, and this genius here has checked in the food, including the stuff I just mentioned. Whatever's left, I want it all back. Now."

"Passover is over. It's all gone."

The Warden becomes flustered and agitated. He points at Negus and says, "Starting tomorrow, you work at the rock up the hill. Hope you meet a shiv with your name on it. Get the hell out of my sight.

Marvin jumps in, "But, Warden!"

Donovan holds his hand up in a stop manner. "Shut up! Try to put one over on me… Hope you like solitary." He turns to Negus and says, "I told you to get out of here." Negus leaves.

Marvin: "Hold on. Please. Let me make up for it."

"How…Working on my retirement plan? Surprised I know? I know everything that goes on here."

Marvin says, "What year is your kid in at Penn State?"

"What the fuck difference does that make?"

"I got an idea," says Marvin.

"Senior," is the warden's reply.

"Perfect. I have some friends in Europe working on this thing called the world wide web. Suppose I get him a job. It will be huge, and he can be in on the ground floor."

The Warden is intrigued. He has heard about this thing called the Internet. "And what am I supposed to do in return?"

"Not much," says Marvin. "Forget about my little indiscretion—I just got carried away.

"Hmmm…And if I look away?"

"So help me, your son will become rich and famous. This web thing will change everything."

The Warden softens a bit. "Let me think about it."

Marvin goes on, "Just one additional little thing…"

The Warden tells him not to push it.

"It's a small matter," replies Marvin.

His reply is angry, "I said I'll think about it."

Undeterred, Marvin says, "It's no big deal…hardly worth mentioning but…"

"What? Dammit!"

"Did you know that Italians like to eat pastrami sandwiches, knishes, and matzo ball soup at Christmas?"

The warden glares at him in disbelief.

"Oh," Marvin goes on, "Would you consider letting Negus stay down here?"

"Maybe I'll consider ways to get you to join him up the hill."

CHAPTER ELEVEN
What Happened to My Shrink?

Therapy sessions using Zoom suck, so I stopped seeing my shrink. I thought things were improving, and I could handle things without him. Covid restrictions were easing, I was knocking it out of the park at work. I loved the freedom of working at home, and I was finally feeling comfortable about myself.

But suddenly, things started to change for the worse. Working from home was ending, and soon it would be back to the daily grind I hated. Ironically, working from home put a real strain on our marriage. Gwen and I kept getting in each other's way, snapping at each other, arguing about the kids, finding genuine and imaginary faults—lots of bickering and many over-the-top fights. The smell of divorce was in the air.

Unexpectedly, the old fears and doubts came back with a vengeance. Sleepless nights, drinking too much, constant worry, the whole collection of neuroses swept in like a rogue wave. It was like the serenity I felt was gone. Okay, I decided, I'll return if he accepts in-office patients.

He did, and I did.

\# \# \#

Over the years, I have not had much success with therapists. I kept kissing frogs looking for the proverbial prince. Whenever I start with a new one, I think about the Larry David show, Curb Your Enthusiasm, and this episode. Larry's sidekick and foil Richard Lewis is complaining about his shrink. It seems that Richard saw his therapist on the beach in Malibu, and the therapist was wearing a Speedo bathing suit. It freaked him out on several levels, including that a man of his age and girth had no business wearing a Speedo. He tells Larry that he can't go back to see him because of that. Larry tells him he's right and needs to find a new therapist. To which Richard Lewis replies, "But oh… the back story." That's always how I felt. A new shrink equals weeks of backstories.

My shrink journey began with someone whose specialty was work-related problems. I worked at a marketing agency, and my boss and one of the owners was Florence Altman, the most intelligent person I had ever met, before or since. But I was restless and wanted to leave the nest to fly on my own, despite loving working for her. I was torn and sought some counsel.

The therapist I saw was so laid back that I often wondered if he was awake or asleep. As soon as he heard that my boss was a woman, we spent session after session probing my relationship with my mother, and it got so narrow a focus and annoying that I dropped him.

Next came the canned soda slurper. The sessions started with him drinking from a can of Coke, or some other beverage, and as he sucked on the straw to the bottom, undeterred, he kept slurping on the straw, with a sound that drove me nuts. As in, "I'd like to talk about—slurp, slurp—this problem I'm having—slurp, slurp—and it's really serious—slurp, slurp."

I couldn't wait to get out of there.

Someone told me about a unique therapist who was extraordinarily successful with patients. But I was warned that he was more than a bit eccentric. Eccentric? The man was an asshole caught in a time warp between Mahatma Gandhi and a Hari Krishna disciple, dressed as though he had just returned from an Ashram. I saw him at the beginning of July, and I'll never forget it was over 90 degrees with a thousand percent humidity. His office was stifling. There was an A/C, but it was off, and all windows were shut. I told him I was too warm and that perhaps he could put the air on. He looked at me as though I had told him to sleep with his sister. He obnoxiously thanked me for being so direct and candid and grudgingly turned on the A/C with a scoff. I got up and left.

The best was Leslie Aronson, a tall, very sharp, take-no-prisoners type woman who was very helpful. What I liked about her was that she called me out when she thought I was full of shit and guided our discussions in productive ways. I loved seeing her down on University Place in the Village. If I got there early enough, I could get the best shawarma and falafel from the Israeli vendor around the corner. Believe it or not, I looked forward to seeing her, but then several things happened. First, while I was pouring my heart out about my life and problems, she would often take out her knitting while we talked. WTF? And while one of my previous shrinks couldn't get past my mother, Leslie couldn't stop focusing on my father—another WTF. I stopped seeing her.

Finally, I came to see Sy Preston and knew immediately that he was the one who could help.

At six foot two, handsome, with wavy black hair, and an unbelievable tan, Sy was the kind of person who, when he walked into a room, stopped conversations. Everyone focused on him. Yet he had no airs and was a down-to-earth kind of guy. Or. So, I thought.

He was a big help and made me see things more clearly. I loved seeing him and benefited from his advice. Ah, but then Covid hit, and sessions on Zoom didn't work for me. We parted ways.

# # #

You already know how difficult things were for me, so I returned to Sy.

I emailed him and asked for an appointment, but something strange happened. Instead of an email response, I received a call from a pleasant-sounding young woman who identified herself as Sy's assistant. Okay, I thought, his practice must have grown. Then she went on to ask all sorts of questions as though I had never been to see him. Stupid questions. Inappropriate questions. Unprofessional questions...do I need to go on? The only smart thing she did was inform me that Sy had moved the office uptown.

Something was amiss. Sy Preston's office was my safe place. A feeling of calm spread over me whenever I walked into his office. In the past, when I booked an appointment, that was enough to make me feel as though a blanket of peace had fallen over me. Not this time.

It must be my imagination, I thought. I probably felt guilty about the hiatus. Okay, I'll relax and see him. He'll help me make things right.

The appointment date arrived. His new office on Park Avenue and 56th Street was not too shabby. The first thing that hit me was that the waiting room had changed; not surprisingly, it was a new office. But the décor threw me off. The peaceful paintings and photographs were gone, and abstract art was in their place. Abstract? It looked like someone had been sick on the walls and decorated it with...never mind. The sedate and comfortable furnishings had given way to loud, obnoxious décor.

Okay, I thought. I've been away for six months. Things have changed since seeing him. What brought on these changes? From feeling calm, relaxed, and at home, I now felt that I had wandered into a cross between a fun house and the set of a 1960s B movie. I suppressed the panic and anger.

As I waited, his office door opened, and a patient walked out. I have shirts and ties older than her, I thought. She looked like she was in her 20s, not the age group I was used to seeing in his office. She smiled in the gentle way a kid smiles at a codger, which I am far from being. This is strange, I thought. In the old days... ha, less than a year ago... he would schedule appointments such that patients did not run into each other. I thought about bolting out.

Before I could, Sy came out and ushered me in.

My British friends had a perfect expression of what I saw and thought. I was fucking gob-smacked. In case you're unfamiliar with the term, it means — according to the dictionary — overwhelmed with wonder, surprise, or shock. His office used to be serene and comfortable, and it now looked like a set from a teeny-bopper film. It gave off the aura of someone trying to be what he was not.

His greeting for me was met with a surprised look on my

face. I stammered, "Doc, what happened? How did your practice turn into…this…this weird funhouse?"

He ignored my question. As he ushered me to the most uncomfortable couch I have ever encountered, he gave his lame explanation. "Look," he said. "Covid changed everything."

My reply was, "No shit?" I asked. "What does that have to do with running a kindergarten?"

With that question, I saw him blink, blush, and become very defensive.

"Look, my former patients wore me out," he said sheepishly.

"What?" I asked him. "You're a therapist! Your patients wore you out? Why didn't you go into another line of work? Maybe construction? What the hell are you talking about? Have you seen a shrink lately?"

I started to say more, but he interrupted me. "My practice was falling apart. Many of my patients were older than I would have liked, and many got seriously ill and permanently stopped coming. A few passed away, and I had to make a change."

He went on, "You don't understand. I became sick and tired of hearing the same lame complaints about their children becoming difficult adults. I want to shout that if you were a loving and decent parent, that would not have happened. In addition, I was sick and tired of hearing about money problems, the pain of aging, sexual dysfunction, and other grievances. I became a therapist to help people, but it became a complaint department. I was bored out of my mind."

"Hold on," I nearly shouted. "That's your damn job. That's what you do, and you get paid well, I might add. What is wrong with you?

He answered, "I'm tired of the senior kvetching and want more contemporary problems, and I want younger patients and more interesting sessions. And New York has tons of young, neurotic, affluent people."

I just stared at him. I couldn't believe what I was hearing. "So, you cut off your relationship with people who came to you for help and spent years in therapy?"

He smiled and said, "Don't be concerned. I'm glad you're back, and we can pick up where we left off. You have at least ten years until I ask you to move on."

He chuckled.

I lost it.

"Sy, I had no idea that one of the lingering side effects of the pandemic was that people…like you…turn into assholes."

I gave him the middle finger salute, headed for the door, and started to make my exit. As I left, he shouted, "You still have to pay for this visit!"

I opened the door, stuck my head back in, and said, "Try and collect, you jerk."

ARTHUR SHAPIRO

CHAPTER TWELVE
The Office Snake

In New York City, it's widely known that people don't change jobs: they change subway stops.

Farrell Smith had a good job working in the mailroom at an ad agency while attending college. His friend Arturo told him about an opening in a marketing agency where he worked. It paid more than the ad agency, but he still would be at the bottom of the feeding chain. Farrell didn't care. He was in his sophomore year at Hunter College, and the job opportunity had a few things going for it. It was two subway stops closer to home, although he didn't give a shit about that. And working at a marketing agency seemed like a step up from advertising, was more interesting. He seemed to have better chances for a full-time job after he graduated.

Farrell grew up in the Bedford-Stuyvesant neighborhood in Brooklyn, also known as Bed-Stuy, a predominantly black neighborhood. His father, Hiram, was a decorated Iraq War veteran and a United States Postal Service supervisor. His mother, Toni—short for Antoinette—was a head nurse at Weill Cornell Surgery Brooklyn Hospital. They raised Farrell with values centered on hard work, honesty, and caring for others. Little did they know that these traits would stand him in good stead at his new job.

Farrell was handsome, six feet tall, pleasant, and friendly. He knew that despite all the gains black men and women had attained, they were not readily accepted. Unlike his white peers, he had to prove himself day after day. He didn't get angry at

135

that. He didn't complain. He just accepted it and strived to overcome it. It was just the way things were, he thought. And fuck them if they didn't see his talent. "Just do your job to the best of your ability," was his father's advice.

He was going from the leading ad agency in the country, if not the world, to a struggling marketing agency that most would consider a step-down. But to Farrell, a small struggling company seemed like a pathway to the future. So, what if he started in the mailroom—all the sweeter to move up and be recognized.

The company was Crosby, McDougall, and Stuart—known as CMS—and had been around since the 1940s. Its heyday was in the 1980s, and by the 2020s it was falling off the map. Nevertheless, they had talented people and the drive to return to their former glory. While their revenue was weak, their reputation was still strong.

Farrell accomplished his goal and his dream. After a year in the mailroom, his talent was recognized, and one of the owners demanded to know why this intelligent, creative kid was doing mailroom stuff when he had so much more to offer. His waspy managers were at a loss to explain and feared being labeled as bigoted. By his junior year at Hunter, his part-time job had gone from the mailroom to project assistance, and he was fast becoming a player at the company. When he graduated, they offered him a full-time job at a good salary, which gave him all the trappings of a rising star. He was now an Associate Project Manager.

# # #

The firm's biggest client was a packaged/processed food company, General Foods International (GFI). It was run by many arrogant, stupid, and horny losers. They cared about after-work drinks and hookups more than the business. Farrell was assigned to work on their business, and even if he didn't fit in, he still did his job. After graduation, he became their lead marketing advisor. His role was to make recommendations based on marketing insights and research. The frat boys hated him for interfering with their faux work in favor of doing the right thing for the business, not to mention their jobs.

On one occasion, a 'genius' brand manager showed Farrell his presentation about how to turn around the failing imitation butter business. He asked Farrell to use marketing research to prove his point of view. Prove his point of view? Farrell explained that marketing research intends to find the truth or the direction objectively and was not meant to be used the way the genius suggested.

In addition, the brand manager's answer to turning the business around was so off base that Farrell laughed his ass off privately and pushed back, recommending an alternative strategy and approach. The brand manager became incensed. "I spent fucking weeks on this. Who the hell are you to tell me it won't work?"

Farrell's answer: "It's off, based on what consumers think. You should reconsider."

"Up yours, boy," was the response. Farrell seriously considered punching him in the face but kept his cool.

You can imagine Farrell's delight when the brand manager was fired for stupidity. More than that, Farrell's reputation at the marketing agency grew. At the GFI, not so much: many felt he was a traitor, and who did he think he was to get the brand manager in trouble? The fact that Farrell could have saved the asshole's job never occurred to the frat boys, whose racism began to show.

His bosses at CMS loved him and protected him from the food fools who demanded his head on a plate. They made it clear that he was as important to the company as their business was. But to placate the food company, they reduced his number of projects while at the same time putting him on other more exciting and profitable businesses. In addition, he was promoted to Senior Project Manager.

CMS's struggle to grow meant that they needed the revenue from the food company, assholes or not. Therefore, they decided they had to have a "rainmaker," someone with super sales ability, a proven track record, and the craftiness to work with them successfully.

They hired Henry Freed, and that's when the trouble began.

# # #

Henry Freed was indeed a rainmaker. He was a senior partner and part-owner of Marketing Facts and Insights, a leading marketing agency whose primary client was General Foods International. The management of Farrell's company salivated at the opportunity to hire him, let him lead that business, and hopefully return them to former excellence.

The owners at CMS opposed 'poaching' Henry; they considered stealing an employee wrong and outside their business values. But when Henry heard about their interest in hiring a hot shot, he did some investigating—snooping actually—and learned that they were paying top dollar, offered a vast performance bonus, and some ownership in the company. Henry took no more than a New York minute to cash out at Marketing Facts and Insights and join CMS.

Henry Freed was a small man in several respects. He had a Napoleon complex at five feet six and a hundred and sixty pounds. And he could have been better-looking. His reputation as a business development executive more than made up for, well, his questionable ethics and manner. It was a no-brainer to have him run the GFI business. They knew him, and he knew them, a perfect arrangement.

The other issue was his reputation for being small-minded, arrogant, and mistreating those who worked for him. Despite their values, CMS management decided to overlook his work style and find a way to channel his sales ability. So, the dilemma the CMS management had to deal with was how to get the most out of Freed and keep their staff from quitting.

That responsibility fell into the lap of one of the owners. Abram Cabell was an old-school Wasp anti-Semite. The solution he sold to his partners was having the black kid become Freed's lead project manager. He said, "The kid has talent, knows GFI, and Jews and Blacks know how to get along."

"What are you saying?" asked the CEO.

Cabell replied, "Come on…Freed is a Jew without values, and Farrell is a black guy with honor. Perfect match."

And so, the team of strange bedfellows was created. Henry was the consummate sales guy, suggesting projects and bringing in business, while Farrell made things happen. But Henry was superficial and paid little attention. His projects cost way more than his proposals, and CMS lost money on almost all of them. Of course, he blamed it all on Farrell.

Cost overruns? Farrell had screwed up the budget. Were project reports late? Farrell hadn't watched the calendar. Objective not addressed. It was Farrell who misunderstood the brief. In all instances, it was Henry's lack of attentiveness to details, superficial understanding of project intents, and submitting a low-cost bid to get the project. Henry Farrell was a lazy piece of shit who only cared about getting the sale, no matter what.

Farrell complained to Cabell about Henry and how he blamed him for his mistakes, minimized his role, and ridiculed him at GFI. He told Cabell that Freed was making his life miserable and couldn't understand his behavior. Weren't they on the same team? Weren't both their salaries and bonuses tied to performance?

When Farrell went to Cabell and asked for advice and help, he was shocked at the response. In his arrogant, obnoxious manner, Cabell suggested: "I'm sure it's not that bad. My mother used to say that when you have a problem, chances are that if you sleep on it, it will be less of a problem the next morning. Get a good night's sleep, and all will be okay tomorrow." Farrell looked at him for a few moments with hate in his eyes. Cabell became nervous and looked away. Without saying a word, still glaring, Farrell left his office.

# # #

That night at dinner with his girlfriend, he bared his burden to her. Her advice was short and to the point: "Quit. You're too talented to work with these crackers. Find something else."

The advice from his parents was similar, but they added, Don't quit until you have something else. "Hopefully, it will come when they need you, so be sure you don't give them more than a two-week notice. If you can, give the fuckers a week."

Farrell's sense of justice loved the recommendations. He started on his resume that night.

A few weeks passed, and Farrell went on a few discreet interviews, and he was surprised at how many headhunters contacted him. All the same, he continued doing his job at CMS, as always.

One day after that, Freed came into his office. It was after six at night, and Farrell was surprised—Freed never came into his office, always summonsing him to his, and after six was a surprise since Freed was always gone by 5:00 to catch his train to Pelham. Okay, thought Farrell, something was up.

"Hey, Henry, to what do I owe the pleasure of your visit?"

Freed was silent and just sat down. He looked nervous.

"Why are you looking for a job?" he blurted out.

"How do you know that?"

"I...uh, was looking for something on your desk the other day, and I saw your resume," was Henry's reply.

Farrell loses it, got up, anger showing. Soon he was right in

Henry's face. "You're a damn liar! There was a resume on my desk, but it was hidden in the bottom drawer under a stack of papers. You rifled through my desk! That makes you a fucking thief. And if you don't like what I just said, you can fire me. But for now, get the hell out of my office."

Henry was shaken up. He started to explain, muttering something about looking for a report, but the look in Farrell's eyes told him to get out quickly. He shut up and left.

Farrell yelled after him, "If I am going to quit, you'll be the last one to know."

# # #

The next day there was unusual activity in the office. Doors opening and closing, private meetings, people in and out of closed doors. It was obvious to Farrell what was happening, and he waited to be approached or summoned. Sure enough, he was told to come to Cabell's office late that afternoon.

Cabell came right to the point. No, how are you? Please sit down.

"What's this about your looking for a new job?"

"Listen, Abram, your hero Henry Freed invaded my privacy, rifled through my desk, discovered my resume, and decided that I must be looking for a new job," was Farrell's reply.

"Well, are you?" asked Cabell.

"I have the right to prepare my resume anytime and for any reason. You, this company, that shithead, don't have the right to invade my privacy."

"Oh yes, we do," said Cabell. "But that's not the point here. We have a right to know if you're planning to leave."

Farrell, trying his best to control himself, replied, "One, I am doing my job to the best of my ability without hesitation, as I have always done. Two, I have not quit, nor have I informed anyone here of an intention to quit. Three, I came to you to tell you how he was making my life miserable and hurting the company by giving projects away without concern about costs and then blaming me for his screw-ups. Your response was to tell me how your mother handled such stress, and I should go home to bed, and it will all be better in the morning. Wow, such profound HR advice. Guess what? It didn't work."

Cabell's face turned red, and he began to sputter. Finally, he managed to say, "How dare you speak to me that way?"

Farrell continued, "You mean after all the things you've done for me? I guess I'm just ungrateful. Tell you what. Why don't you fire me? Give me my severance package. I'll leave today, and you can get someone else to finish the reports to GFI that are due the day after tomorrow. I'll go pack my things." He started to leave.

"Wait," said Cabell. "Come back. Sit down, please. I'll be right back."

He left and returned ten minutes later with the senior partner and Henry Freed. They discussed the situation for the next hour, and apologies flowed from Freed's mouth like honey from a hive. Assurances were made that things would be different, Farrell would have a special salary review, his bonus adjusted upward.

Farrell barely uttered a word, and after they were done, he

smiled in a friendly manner and indicated that he had reports to write and would like to get back to work. Handshakes and satisfied looks all around—Cabell even gave him a friendly pat on the back.

Back at his desk, the phone rang, and it was the employment and job placement agency he was hoping to hear from. The vice president he was dealing with was excited and told him that the YSW agency, among the best in the business, would like him to come back for another interview, this time with the president. They set a date for the following week.

# # #

Three weeks later, he got a call from the headhunter telling him the job was his and when could he start? His answer was that it would be best to give two weeks' notice, but he'd prefer to start immediately. They agreed to two weeks.

Farrell would always remember the next day as among the best in his life. As soon as Cabell arrived in his office, Farrell was right there and asked to see him.

Cabell said, "Can't it wait until I have my coffee?"

"Sure," said Farrell. "In addition to your cream and sugar, you can stir with my resignation." He turned around and walked out.

Within half an hour, Cabell, Freed, and the other owners called Farrell to the conference room to discuss his announcement.

"How can you do this to us after all we have done for you? Quite frankly, we have given you, a minority, opportunity after opportunity that you would have never gotten elsewhere," lamented Cabell.

Calm on the outside but burning inside, Farrell said, "Yes, you gave me many opportunities, and I paid you back with hard work and creativity. I gave more than I got. You made me the zookeeper for a lying, nasty, dishonest turd." He glared at Freed and said, "I'm done here, and while I was taught to be a gentleman and not burn bridges, in this case, I will be out of here in two weeks. One word from any of you, and I will leave now." Silence was the response. Farrell got up and left the room.

# # #

Farrell stayed the two weeks and did his work as though nothing had happened. But he spoke to no one and did not attend any meetings or presentations. He joined YSW and immediately felt at home. In the ten years that followed, he became a superstar and ultimately became executive vice president in charge of all consumer business clients.

Henry Freed struggled after Farrell's departure. All his projects ran into difficulty and continued to lose money, but with no one to blame. Cabell and the other owners lost their patience with him, and one day, they decided to audit his expense account. The irregularities—no one wanted to say cheating—were such that when they confronted him and threatened to prosecute, he agreed to resign without severance and forgo his annual bonus. He went off to Hollywood and convinced a studio that he could predict the success or failure of a new film based on audience reactions. That idea also failed miserably. He disappeared.

As to CMS, within a year of Farrell's departure, on the verge of bankruptcy, they sold the company, based on its name and history, for less than ten cents on the dollar. They were gone, and Cabell had to settle for a job that even his mother would have hated.

Oh, and by the way, Farrell's job at YSW was five subway stops away from where he lived. And that didn't even matter as much as it might have because the company provided him with a car and driver.

CHAPTER THIRTEEN
The Narcissist

Aldo Parnell, born Aaron Pachmann, was not always a narcissist. He started as a gifted and talented arrogant slob and, through circumstances and temperament, gradually became a world-class pathological narcissist. And a world-class asshole too.

His upbringing might have had something to do with it. The son of an Orthodox Jewish family living in Borough Park, Brooklyn, he hated being Jewish and yearned to escape his family to enter the world of the rich and famous. He was preoccupied with thoughts of power and success, surrounded himself with people he felt were important, and had an aura of entitlement. Early signs of what was to come.

There were constant battles in the Pachmann household. He detested his family and upbringing, aspired to be famous, and admired himself. But none of his aspirations could be realized while living in Borough Park. His parents insisted that he go to a Yeshiva, which he did until graduating from elementary school. But unknown to his parents, he applied and was accepted to The Bronx High School of Science. Somehow, with the help of a friendly neighborhood rabbi, he convinced his parents that this was a wise move.

Several things happened in the four years at Bronx Science. He hung out with the few kids whose desires and values he shared and brought his virtues forward: self-importance, arrogance, and a permanent focus on exploiting others for his own gain. His sneers and ridicule of other students earned him the reputation of someone to be avoided.

The other seminal event in his life was the discovery of the art and self-expression of the camera. Despite his arrogance, he was good at photography. In addition, art, architecture, and, surprising even him, literature and writing rounded out the areas of his teenage focus. By the time he graduated, he had decided to pursue a life in advertising. You can imagine what took place in the Pachmann household when he announced that, at age eighteen, he was going to the Parsons School of Design and leaving home. By this point, his father was relieved to be rid of the arrogant putz, as he called him, and turned his back while his son packed. His mother tried to resolve matters, but Aaron/Aldo's arrogance proved too much for her love. So she focused her attention on the other two children and moved on.

So, in 1980, Aldo Parnell, nee Aaron Pachmann, left Borough Park, Brooklyn, and took residence in a tenement on the Lower East Side. While attending Parsons, he survived by various part-time jobs and creating portrait photos of children. He was miserable, but his arrogance did not wane. On the contrary, he looked down on his customers, and his narcissism grew, as did his nastiness.

In his senior year, he got a job in the mailroom at an up-and-coming advertising agency that had as its mission the revolutionizing of the ad business. Unlike in the past, when relationships and the 'right contacts' ruled the industry, this forward-thinking agency focused on creativity. The golden age of advertising creativity was blossoming. And Aldo knew this was his calling. His destiny. His future.

\# \# \#

After graduating, he was offered a job at another neophyte ad agency. This time, he was one of a few newbie hotshots building a reputation for creative talent. After a few years, Aldo and a colleague decided to leave and start their own agency. Aldo was the creative head—both art director and copywriter, while his partner was responsible for bringing in business and managing clients. One of their first clients was a candy company. It was fitting since Aldo had gained considerable weight.

Aldo Parnell's appearance was consistent with his narcissism and mean-spirited demeanor. He was not a particularly good-looking man at five feet ten, prematurely bald, and with a perpetual sneer. He could give a shit, and of course, his self-importance mattered to him.

The fact that he was approaching 280 pounds, and could only wear triple XL clothing, didn't faze him a bit. He thought his creativity and strategic thinking were more important than his appearance. Besides, he considered clients fools fortunate to have his skills working on their business. So, who cares what he looked like?

All this background brings us to a particular event after he and his partner had worked on the Y&R Candy Company business for five years. The company was worried about the growing weight concerns of the country and looked to Aldo and his partner for help with their dilemma—how to grow their business in this health-conscious new environment.

Aldo's presentation of a new campaign reflected his essential arrogance. "Fuck the fools who worry about weight. Your products are about enjoyment and indulgence. Guilty pleasures. Target those people." That was his advice. He punctuated his presentation by opening a pound bag of their candy and pouring the contents into his mouth as he consumed the entire package. An obnoxious display.

The result was that the Y&R people left aghast. Further, it suddenly dawned on them that this so-called creative genius was anything but, and given his morbid obesity, he didn't understand the changes in consumer attitudes. Besides, who wants an overweight, arrogant schmuck handling their communications? Aldo's company was fired the next day.

His partner was livid. "What the hell is wrong with you?" he demanded. "Do you know how hard I've worked to keep them happy and increase our business? You fucked up."

Aldo just stared at him and said, "Who needs them? For years they have challenged our creativity...mine...I say good riddance. We're doing well with other accounts."

"Other accounts? Do you realize that they're the biggest candy company in the country, and I was working on getting them to make us the development agency for their exclusive new products? Do you also realize I walk behind you like a circus porter, cleaning up the shit you drop like an elephant? Your talent is excellent, but like a cow that gives a bucket of milk and then kicks over the bucket, your creativity is destroyed by your obnoxious personality. We're done. The partnership is over. Lawyers will settle our so-called relationship."

Aldo was delighted. He long felt that his partner stifled his creative talents to curry favor with clients. At last, he thought I can start my own agency and be the master of my own fate.

The Aldo Parnell Company was born.

# # #

At last, Aldo achieved his goal of being rich and famous. For whatever reason, his agency became the most desirable in the business. Clients flocked to him. Despite his girth and demeanor, he was seen as an eccentric but highly creative character. His high-paying clients included a veritable who's who in financial services, health care, automotive, electronics, fashion, and cosmetics. To handle the business, he hired top-notch talent, overpaid them, and verbally abused and ridiculed them. But for the most part, they stayed and took it, just like the expression, "Money talks, and nobody walks."

At one client presentation, Aldo met Charlie Pine, an up-and-coming marketing executive. They were opposites: Charlie's charm and people orientation was remarkable. Unfortunately, shortly after they got acquainted, Charlie left his company and took a senior position with a spirits and wine company responsible for the European business. Aldo could care less about Charlie's departure but made a mental note to follow his career and bide his time.

Charlie was indeed a star. At six feet tall, with blond hair, blue eyes, and a fantastic smile accompanied by a jovial—but serious—manner, he made it easy for distributors and customers all over Europe to love doing business with him. As a result, his success and notoriety attracted the attention of the owners and management of the company, and they wanted Charlie's expertise in the headquarters office.

Stillman Spirits Company was not the largest in the alcohol industry but the most influential. Charlie was assigned to the marketing department run by Adam Chadwick, a rising star at the company. Their relationship was not founded on anything other than mutual respect and admiration. They were colleagues, not supervisor and employee.

One thing that bonded them was their common enemy—the president of their division. He had a love-hate relationship with Charlie, and even though Adam was his boss, the president kept going around him to control Charlie's work. The result was that Charlie spent many hours with Adam, commiserating about his treatment and laughing about it.

Things changed appreciably when one of the owners met a Scotch entrepreneur looking for a relationship with Stillman. He was seeking help developing and marketing his unique whisky. It became clear to all at the company that Charlie and Adam had been instructed to make things happen, and everyone else, regardless of their position, was to stay out of their way. The owner had grand plans for the whisky and the entrepreneur and was determined to make the product and brand the star of their portfolio. Charlie and Adam were ecstatic; they worked well together. Since Adam ran the marketing department with other responsibilities and Charlie reported to him, Adam gave him the lead and asked to be kept informed.

# # #

The Aldo Parnell Company continued to thrive and gain notoriety. Despite his brutal ways, Aldo was a gifted advertising guy with extraordinary creative talent. Clients wrote off his strange demeanor. As one put it, "Aldo is an asshole and says and does things I would fire most ad people for. He's rude, boorish, and mean. But his ideas, from strategy to execution, are top-notch." An advertising writer for a significant business publication put it differently, "His work is partly great and mainly bullshit. Clients are intimidated by his attitude and applaud his creativity because they are afraid to be seen as philistines should they dare to reject his campaigns. One day he will self-destruct."

Prophetic words.

By the late 1990s, Aldo and his agency were on a roll. In addition to the creative work, Aldo had gotten involved with business development and client management. To support him, particularly regarding new clients, Aldo had seven assistants: a few did administrative work, but most scoured publications and the emerging internet to identify prospects. That's how they found Charlie again. Even more interesting to Aldo was the opportunity to work with the Stillman company and start by making their new Scotch product a success. A meeting with Charlie was arranged.

Charlie was no fool. He could smell bullshit a mile away, and Aldo often reeked of it. At the same time, Charlie realized Aldo's talent was not just outstanding; his focus on innovation and advertising that could break through the clutter was precisely what this new brand needed. They spent some time together, and Charlie decided to have Aldo meet and present to Adam, whose decision to hire Aldo's agency would be his. They arranged a meeting with Charlie, Adam, and a few brand managers.

Several things happened at that first meeting. It was scheduled for two o'clock, and by two fifteen, still no sign of Aldo. Just as Adam decided to leave and return to his office, the receptionist announced that the agency had arrived. In walked Aldo with an entourage of sycophants, most of whom looked like they were still in high school. No apologies for being late. Introductions were made while they set up their presentation. Adam was doing a slow burn but waited patiently for their pitch.

And a fantastic pitch it was.

All that was missing were bells, whistles, dogs in tutus, dancing ponies, and the Rockettes. Aldo and his people went all-out to show their capabilities and how they would approach building the new Scotch brand. They had made films of Scotland and the distillery, an array of traditional Gaelic culture, including artifacts, old parchment paper, statues, and a fascinating lecture on Scottish things, delivered by a man in kilts and with a thick Scottish accent. It was impressive.

Aldo was most solicitous toward Adam, knowing that he had to win him over if they were to be assigned the business. Adam saw right through that but felt, what the hell, let's see what he comes back with. Not one to focus on appearances, Adam was nevertheless put off by Aldo's weight, which he guessed at over 300 pounds.

The other off-putting thing was how Aldo dressed. Stillman

was very particular about appearances, which Adam thought ridiculous, but the owners insisted on conservative dress. He thought that was their way of demonstrating they were no longer bootleggers or gangsters. Yet, here was an agency owner dressed in cutoff white jean shorts (in winter) with a humongous white shirt. He looked like a cross between a polar bear and the Loch Ness monster. Leaning down, he whispered to Charlie, "No way will I bring this clown forward to meet management and the owners." Charlie responded, "Let's see what they come back with. You know that Junior loves the offbeat." Junior, as he was known behind his back, was the third generation of the Stillman family.

The meeting ended with the Stillman people briefing the agency on their expectations. Adam couldn't wait to get out of there.

A few weeks passed, and the agency returned with a campaign that even Adam thought was terrific. It was, as the Brits say, "spot on." Adam had to get approval for his decision from management and the owners to move forward. They usually trusted him and agreed with his choices. But this time, it was different. Typically, new creative was presented by the agency, with the head of marketing—Adam, in this case—setting the stage with why he selected the agency and why he felt the communications would excel. He was concerned that one look at Aldo, accompanied by the man's sheer arrogance, would doom the advertising and maybe him. But Adam had guts and decided to proceed anyway.

To his surprise—no, make that shock—they all loved the work and supported Adam's decision to proceed.

As the meeting broke up, amidst high fives and atta boys,

Junior asked Adam to meet him in his office. Junior had two things to say when he arrived, "I love the campaign, but I never want to see that fat egotist again. Are we clear?"

Adam, a bit put off, wanted to say, "Yes, my liege," but didn't think that comment would go over well. Instead, he said, "Sure."

The brand was launched and took off like a rocket. Unfortunately, Junior and the family decide that the booze business was not for them—and stupidly chose to sell the company so they could enter the entertainment industry. That dumb decision and its abject stupidity turned out to be a disaster. But that's a story for another time.

# # #

Everything changed by 2005. Aldo had sold his agency to an adverting conglomerate and made a ton of money. Stillman Spirits and Wine ceased to exist. Aldo was given free rein to run his agency as he saw fit, provided he made his financial objectives. Remarkably he lost over 200 pounds, was down to 150, and bought his suits and furnishings from Saville Row. He became a man of style. His narcissistic attitude and demeanor accelerated even more.

The business was going through the roof, and Aldo needed help managing the company. He decided to hire Charlie Pine and make him the president. The fact of the matter was that Aldo was getting bored and looking to expand his horizons by ingratiating himself with celebrities who offered the opportunity to leverage their names by developing food and beverage products, cosmetics, soft drinks, and alcohol. Charlie managed the day-to-day business while Aldo ran off, kissing well-known and potentially lucrative asses.

Charlie brought in his pal Adam Chadwick as a consultant and hired others he had worked with to be on his staff. Aldo was unhappy with these people and arrived unexpectedly at many meetings despite his supposed removal from the day-to-day business. He behaved as a spoiled child who delights in pulling the wings off a fly. He dominated the discussions, changed the agendas, and regally ran the show. One time and one time only, Adam had the temerity to disagree with Aldo over one of his suggestions. When he did that, everyone in the room went silent and put their heads down, waiting for an explosion. Aldo glared at him and was about to detonate when one of his assistants came into the conference room and informed him that Diane Sawyer, a new prospect, was on the phone.

He left the meeting with the words, "This ain't over."

After he was gone, one of his lackeys said, "Adam, no one contradicts him. What is wrong with you? Can't you keep quiet and go along?"

Adam's reply: "Fuck that. I'm not wired that way, and I do not worship at the altar of narcissistic assholes. I get paid to give advice and recommendations if that offends him… too damn bad." With that, he got up and left.

The next day at another meeting, Aldo barged in and informed Adam that while he may have been a hotshot at Stillman, now he was just another consultant and needed to learn his place. In addition, he didn't like how Adam dressed. Although he did love his watch. He repeatedly invoked his admiration for the watch as though he wanted it as compensation for Adam's outspokenness. Adam stared at him with an unsettling look and said, "Listen closely… I have two choices here… I can go Brooklyn on you and teach you a lesson you will need six weeks to recover from, or I can tell you to fuck off, kiss my ass, and I'm gone. I choose the latter." With that, he gave Aldo the middle finger salute and left.

# # #

No one can now recall the turning point in Aldo's career and fortune. In later years, Adam took credit for Aldo's fall based on the time he told him off. But that wasn't it.

What happened was this: Aldo's arrogance got the better of him. His sneers and ridicule of clients, not to mention the "I know better approach," began to backfire. He was not inclined to move things forward as much as he pushed for changes that had less to do with growing a client's business than with polishing Aldo's ego. Failure after failure, misstep after misstep, began to take a toll. Ironically, the more he tried, the more he failed. And the crazier he became.

Some examples: he advised and pushed for an auto client to get out of the truck and utility vehicle business when that market was changing exactly in their favor, and the company almost went bankrupt as a result. He was privy to the secret recipe of a famous soft drink company and pushed them to reveal pieces of the recipe, which caused the CEO to be fired by the board of directors. The coup de grace came when he pushed a juice company to change its packaging, making consumers wonder about changes to the juice itself. His public explanation via YouTube became the laughingstock of the marketing and advertising world. The result: the agency conglomerate that owned his company closed Aldo Parnell Company, paid off Aldo, and told him to get lost.

He left the country, found a wealthy European heiress, married her, returned to his former massive weight, and vanished into obscurity.

Sometimes, the decent folks win, and the narcissists lose.

Maybe because the apple bites back.

THE BIG APPLE BITES BACK

CHAPTER FOURTEEN
Short Takes

THE CAB RIDE

The dinner reservation was for 7:15. We called Lyft for a ride from the Upper East Side to Midtown. The Lyft app indicated 5 minutes, but from the GPS location, there was no way the car could get here in under 15. We got a cab right away and took the FDR Drive downtown.

As we entered the highway, the driver, a Korean man in his 40s, reached over and took a cooked ear of corn out of a bag, then proceeded to devour it, munching happily with one hand as he drove with the other. He was a good driver, and we weren't concerned about safety. I marveled at his skill and especially his hunger. It's a tough job driving a cab, especially on a Friday night in June. I guess you get your food breaks when you can.

We entered the drive at 79th Street, and by the time he got off two exits away at 53rd Street, all that was left in his hand was a corn cob. He carefully placed it back in the bag and wiped his hands with a napkin. I swear I might have heard a sigh of contentment.

Despite the partition, I leaned forward and said, "That must have been a delicious ear of corn." He looked at me through the rear-view mirror and smiled. "My father is from North Korea and taught me that when you're hungry, the taste doesn't matter."

He then proceeded to take out another ear of corn and eat it with the same enthusiasm as the first. And, in less than five crosstown blocks, it was gone as we talked about what life must be like in North Korea.

I over-tipped him.

PHONE SEX

Bob dials. Nancy picks up. Nancy has a soft, sexy voice with just the hint of an accent.

NANCY: Hello Bob. How have you been?

BOB (Nervously): How did you know it was me?

NANCY: Caller ID, silly.

BOB: Oh, I keep forgetting that.

NANCY: It's always great to hear from you, Bob. What would you like? What are you in the mood for? We had fun when you were in last time.

BOB: Yes, we did. You know, I really don't like this phone stuff. I'd rather come there in person.

NANCY: That would be okay. Can you come over?

BOB: Hmmm. Well, not tonight. I'm in a bit of a hurry.

NANCY: Okay. What shall it be? The usual?

BOB: No, I'm in the mood for something different.

NANCY: Are you sure? The last time it was different, you weren't too happy. Remember?

BOB: That's because it was way too exotic for me.

NANCY: Give me some idea of what you might like tonight.

BOB: Do you have anything new you could recommend?

NANCY: Yes. There is. Something special. But you said you were in a hurry, should we do something very quick…

BOB: No. [pause] Let me think…

NANCY: Bob, would you like to call back?

BOB: No, I really want something to…you know…enjoy. Oh, the hell with it. Let's do something special. It's time I let go and went for it. Let's do it!

NANCY: Okay. [pause] One Szechuan double-cooked pork, extra spicy…white or brown rice?

THE SHOPLIFTER

Dan and Donna Ryan, each in their early 30s, often went shopping together. Dan had a thing for Duane Reade, which Donna couldn't understand. "Why Duane Reade or CVS all the time? D'Agostino's or Shoprite has what we need; why do we always go to the drugstore chains?"

Dan was usually noncommittal and muttered something about a better selection of stuff and that he just liked those stores more. Their marriage had become rocky, and Donna didn't need another fight with him. So she usually just went along.

On this visit to a nearby Duane Reade, one of the largest in NYC, they found the marquis signage had changed to new owners, Walgreens. Dan suggested they each go shopping for what they needed, and Donna wandered off. Then so did Dan.

Ten minutes later, Dan was leaning against a wall, a police officer handcuffing him.

This was Officer Wax, an NYC veteran cop with close to 30 years on the job. He'd seen and heard everything and couldn't wait for retirement.

"I hate to do this, but they have a zero-tolerance rule for shoplifters, and they caught you red-handed."

Dan's shaky voice answered, "But officer... it was an oversight, an accident. I meant to

put it in my wife's basket, but she was at the other end of the store, and I walked out, forgetting about it. A mistake."

"I'm sorry," said Wax. "You look honest to me, but the manager insists. Wants to make an example of you."

Just then, Donna walked up, saw Dan handcuffed, dropped the packages she was holding and became distraught.

"What's going on," she wailed. "Dan, why did he handcuff you?"

Dan replied that it was all a mistake. Donna wanted to know, "Officer, are you arresting my husband?"

Wax replied, "Afraid so, Ma'am. The charge is shoplifting."

Donna said, "What? You must be joking. What did he shoplift? Why would he? We were shopping together. Dan, what's going on?"

Dan looked sheepishly at the ground. Officer Wax produced a small package and showed it to Donna.

"They caught him on video leaving the store with this item in his pocket."

Donna looked at it closely and was shocked. "That's a box of condoms. Why would he...? Dan, why did you steal a box of condoms? We don't use condoms, I'm on...the...pill." Suddenly, a look of understanding crossed her face. "Why, you son of a bitch!"

Dan tried to explain.

Donna interrupted and exploded, "Explain? Officer, lock this man up!"

THE ATTITUDE SCHOOL

Have you ever wondered why the people who are supposed to help you act like assholes? You know, the customer service rep you get on the phone, the receptionist at your doctor's office, the checkout clerk at the store, or the snot-nosed host or hostess at a restaurant, among others. Well, some of them were born arrogant and nasty, but many went to a special NYC school to learn their "craft."

Let's visit the school. Kenton Bean, a mean-spirited and tough asshole, runs it. And bully. His school is called Kenton's Klan. Get the picture?

Gloria Vasquez is a lovely, pleasant, and mild-mannered single mom in need of a job. She signed up with Kenton to learn how to become a restaurant hostess. It has become a culture shock for her.

She stands at a makeshift podium, waiting for instructions. "Okay," says Kenton, "Where's your gum and your smartphone?"

"I didn't think I needed them, Mr. K," is her reply.

"Of course, you do. How else can you be in control? Keep going."

"Good evening. Do you have a reservation?"

"No. No. Make them wait, keep looking at the computer, your mobile phone. Don't respond until they seem annoyed. Ask them if their entire party is here, and if they say no, tell them to stand aside. If they say yes, pretend you didn't hear and keep looking at the screens. Got it?"

"I think so," says Gloria, "but why not just seat them?"

"Because," says Kenton, "Desirable New York restaurants are supposed to be snooty. Do you want to work at a diner or a first-class spot?"

"Okay," answers Gloria, more than a bit confused.

"Let's move on," says Kenton. He turns his attention to Alondra, who wants to learn how to be a customer service rep. "Alondra, what are the basic rules of customer service operators?"

Alondra says in a shaky, nervous voice, "Number one, always sound like you don't care what the problem is. Number two, don't worry about being rude..." She starts to cry and says, "Why do I have to be rude? Why can't I help people? That's what the job is about, isn't it?"

"I don't think of it as rudeness. It's meeting expectations. They expect us to have an attitude."

"What about all the stuff I read about why companies need good customer service?"

"No such thing. That's just marketing crap. Companies pay us to teach you to be tough. If you treat people nicely, they take advantage. Let's keep going...Samantha, you're a receptionist at a doctor's office."

"Okay," says Samantha.

Kenton pretends to be a patient entering the doctor's office. "Pay attention...Hello, I have an appointment."

"What is your name?" asks Samantha.

"No, no, no!" shrieks Kenton. "You do not ask that right away. Make him wait while you finish texting your friend."

"But what if you, uh, he, is sick?"

"It doesn't matter," snaps Kenton. "It's about you. I don't understand you. You're looking for work but don't seem to be absorbing what I'm teaching you. Come on, people."

He looks around the room and calls on Alondra. "Let's try again. You are behind the checkout counter at a CVS Pharmacy. I walk up to pay. What's the first thing you say to me?"

"Drop dead?"

"Now, we're getting somewhere."

DIRECTIONS

Visitors to NYC frequently complain about how difficult it is to get the locals to provide directions. Most think it's because New Yorkers are rude. That may be true to some degree, but the main reason is that most New Yorkers often have no sense of direction or don't know. So, rather than say, "Gee, I don't know how to get there," the response follows: ignore the question, mumble, "I don't know," or silently glare at the direction asker.

Surely, you have heard the joke about a tourist who is lost

in NYC. A man from the Midwest seems to be trying to get around The City and keeps getting lost. Each time he stops someone and asks for directions, he is rebuffed, ignored, or worse. But he presses on. Finally, he stops a man in the street and says, "Can you tell me how to get to the Museum of Modern Art, or should I go fuck myself?"

THE MARIACHI BAND

It was eleven o'clock in the morning, and the subway was not crowded. When the train came to the station, a man got on. Not particularly big, but a scowl and a look of anger on his face. From his appearance and dress, he was obviously a construction worker who appeared to have fallen on hard times and blamed the world for his problems. Damn immigrants, blacks, and Latinos were getting the best jobs, and he had to suck 'hind tit,' was how he saw it. He thought, Trump may be a world-class asshole, but he's on the right path. Before long, white Americans would be the losers. The fact that he was a first-generation American whose family had emigrated from Eastern Europe was an irony he couldn't see or understand.

He took a seat and got lost in thought.

At the next stop, a family got on. Five kids and their worn-out-looking mother, all of whom were black. Except for one teenager, the kids were young and rambunctious — defined as high-spirited, boarding on boisterous. Instead of sitting, they ran around the poles in the car, bumped into people, shouted at each other, then started to throw things around.

The man was watching this behavior and getting angry, no, make that livid. Just then, one of the kids threw something at another, but it hit the man on the head, and the intended receiver ran into him. He shouted to them, "Sit the fuck down and behave yourselves!" The mother got angry, but the man yelled at her before she could say something, "Why don't you teach your rug rats how to behave in public? This is not your home!"

She glared at him and said, "Shut up, you racist piece-o-shit. Don't you dare talk to me like that, and how dare you yell at my kids?"

"If you had any decency, you would teach your kids how to behave," said the man. "Good thing your man isn't here, I'd kick the shit outta him."

Now the encounter had escalated significantly. Despite the rapid movement of the train, the mother got up and started to move toward the man sitting across from her. The teenage daughter joined her.

The man was staring at them with a nonchalant look on his face that turned into a threatening smirk. "Come on, bitches, I never hit a woman before, but I think I'll enjoy this." He got up.

As they squared off, several things happened. The train started to slow as it got to the next station, and the momentum caused all of them to lose their balance and fall back into their seats. The train stopped, and the antagonists started screaming at each other. The doors opened, and nervous passengers rushed out of the car for safety while half a dozen people pulled out their smartphones and started filming, hoping to have a submission to a local TV station. The confrontation had escalated, and danger was in the air.

Just as they were ready to go after each other, four Mexican musicians, a Mariachi Band, entered the subway car with their instruments and started playing La Bamba.

The mother, daughter, and the man looked at the band, then at each other, and they all started to laugh.

Confrontation averted.

THE WINNER

Victor Vasquez is the office clown and prankster. The tricks he has pulled off over the years have become office legends. We're not talking about your everyday April Fool's tricks. Oh no, his have always been over the top, partly amusing, unless you were the target of his ruses.

His pranks ranged from simple to elaborate. There was the time, for example, when he bought a second dual remote for the TV in the conference room. He kept changing the monitor's image while the presenter talked.

Or the time he put his hand palm down on a table and balanced a full glass of water on the back of his hand. He then bet a co-worker they couldn't balance a glass on both hands simultaneously. He helped him put the glasses in place. As soon as the glasses were balanced, he walked away. His target had to spill the water all over the place to get up.

This went on for years. His bosses tolerated his pranks because he was a top performer, and even they were amused by his seemingly harmless fun.

One day, they had had enough and demanded he cut it out or look for another job. And, so, he stopped for two or three years. Everyone was relieved, but Victor just bided his time, looking to pull off the big one.

The opportunity came.

He and Jane were having lunch in the cafeteria and talking about the lottery ticket they and Harry had bought together. Victor had just finished explaining a trick he had in mind for Harry.

"Okay, so you'll go along?" asked Victor.

Jane told him she was reluctant because the idea seemed cruel. To which Victor replied, "Trust me, I won't let it get out of hand. Just a little practical joke. It works better if you're involved. I'll come clean after a few minutes. I promise. It won't get out of hand."

She looked up and saw Harry coming their way. "Here he comes. Okay, I'll go along. But remember, you promised."

Harry took a seat at the table and asked them, "What's up, guys? I don't suppose our numbers came in last night, did they?" He laughed.

Victor replied in a hushed voice, "Shhh! Lower your voice. Jane and I were just about to go looking for you. We need to figure out what to do, how to play it."

"What?" asked Harry.

"Keep your voice down, and don't react to what I'm going to say. Our numbers hit. Big time."

Harry got very excited. "What? How much?"

"Twelve million."

"Ohmygod!" said Harry, in the loudest whisper voice ever.

"That's four million each! Two after taxes! You have no idea what this means. What problems and stress that money will cure. Hallelujah. Thank you, Lord." He got up, and before they could say a word, he said, "I'll be right back." He ran off.

Jane tried to stop him and shouted, "Wait a minute. Don't go!" But he was gone. To Victor, she said, "This is not good."

"It's okay," he said. "Probably went to call his wife. We'll tell him when he gets back. Don't worry. He's a good sport."

Fifteen minutes later, Peggy, their boss, came over to them.

She was livid. "So, do the two of you also want to tell me off?

"What?" asked Victor.

"No! What are you talking about?" asked Jane.

"Harry just stormed into my office," Peggy said. "He told me that the three of you hit the New York lottery and told me what a bitch I am… spilled coffee on my computer and quit. He said you two might do the same."

"Peggy, it was a practical joke," said Jane. "Before we could tell him, he ran off."

"So sorry," Victor added. "I'll try to make it right."

"Don't bother. I never liked that bastard, anyhow." She started to leave but turned back and got in Victor's face.

"By the way, Victor, your prankster days are over in this company. You can join Harry at the unemployment office."

CHAPTER FIFTEEN
Author's Note — From Sidewalk to Sand

At the beginning of this book, I mentioned that we moved to Rancho Mirage, California, after our lives as New Yorkers. That was in November 2021. It's our next chapter, and semi-retirement allows me to focus on important things to me…stories about my hometown of NYC. And other stories too.

Do I miss the Big Apple? Yes and no.

I miss the theatre (mainly off and off-off Broadway) and strolling to and from dinner. I don't miss the wide range of positive and negative attitudes, the drama, and the constant changes, not all of which have been for the good.

But after 'none-of-your-business' how many years I spent there (basically my whole life), it was time for us to leave the Northeast winters and spend our golden years in warmth and comfort. And little to no humidity.

So, the first thing I need to tell you is that in the two years since we moved out to Coachella Valley, New York had no snow, not a drop, in 2022. Out in the desert this past winter, we had unprecedented rain (in the frigging desert!), temperatures in the low 60s compared to the norm of 70 degrees, and tons of snow in the surrounding mountains—more than in the most memorable snowy seasons.

Don't get me wrong: we love it here. You're probably thinking, "Let's see what he says when it's 120° outside." Well, we are prepared for it. We'd rather take the dry heat than the slush and splash of an NYC winter. But as lifelong New Yorkers, it's more than a little "culture shock."

Allow me to describe some elements of that difference.

Let's start with the basics. Grocery shopping: supermarkets in Manhattan are small. How small? So small that you must go outside to change your mind. So small that aisles are limited by customer size and weight. It was not unusual to hear this announcement: "Attention! Customer stuck in aisle #4. Bring the lard."

In fairness, however, it's the difference between living in a city as opposed to a suburb. Imagine our surprise the first time we walked into a Ralph's or Gelson's. We gawked at these cavernous stores that looked like they were built over a football field.

On one occasion, we walked through this behemoth Ralph's for an hour. Totally exhausted, we headed for the checkout, only to realize that we had forgotten to buy eggs. When we learned that eggs were at the other end of the store, we looked at each other and said, "Forget it. We'll eat breakfast out."

About people differences. This great country has many regions, each of which has its unique culture, values, and even language. For example, we often think of southern hospitality, the laid-back west coast, the special New England 'twang,' and so on.

Of course, the New York City area (including the suburbs) has its own culture and language, influenced by history (the melting pot), the urban density, the hustle and bustle, and more. Think of the scene in Midnight Cowboy, as Dustin Hoffman (the New Yorker) and Jon Voight (from the South) are crossing a crowded Broadway Street, and Hoffman disregards traffic and is almost hit. He yells to a cab that nearly runs him over, "Hey. I'm wawking heyr."

Now don't get me wrong, I love NY, always have, and always will. But it's fun and more than a bit interesting to think about the people differences between NYC and the desert.

The difference in personality between Californians and New Yorkers is best seen by talking to a local customer service representative. When you hang up and say thanks, a call in NY is usually met with a bored, semi-grumpy, "Sure, whatever." Out here, the same thank you signoff is met with a cheerful, "Of course."

Let me tell you the story of our first night at Rancho Mirage. We arrived in mid-November, and thanks to the distance and the upcoming Thanksgiving holiday, our "stuff" was not due for over two weeks. So, we planned to have a bed, a table to eat on, and other "we'll make do" necessities.

We shipped some stuff out via FedEx but forgot the pillows. "No worries," said my wife, Marlene. "Bed, Bath, and Beyond has same-day delivery." So, as we waited at the airport to leave, she ordered them with the understanding that they would arrive that night.

Nine hours later, we arrived, saw no pillows, and waited and waited for the delivery. Marlene called the store just before closing time and was told by the assistant manager, "We're sorry, we don't have same-day delivery, despite what it says online. You'll have to come by the store tomorrow."

Marlene patiently explained the situation but to no avail. We decided to make do and planned to use sofa pillows for the night. A half-hour later, the bell rang, and the assistant manager was standing outside with pillows. We were shocked. She said, "I know what it's like to spend your first night uncomfortable...so welcome to California." She added, "You were on my way home, so I thought I would drop by with these."

Blown away does not begin to describe our reaction. No way this would have happened in NYC. Welcome to California, for sure.

Food and dining: what we love about dining out in the desert is eating outdoors without having to chain Marlene's pocketbook to the table. The unpretentious atmosphere we have experienced almost always includes farm-fresh ingredients and innovation. The California cuisine, Italian, Mexican, and Thai foods all, in my opinion, are on par or better than the Big Apple. And as dog owners, we appreciate the opportunity to occasionally bring Lucy with us without a maître d' asking us in a faux French accent, "Does your dog bite?"

We have not had a chance to sample the desert steakhouses, but I bet they are like those in New York. Oh, and this transplanted NYer is a huge fan of In-N-Out Burger—nothing like it back where I come from. I have a friend and client who, on trips to the West Coast, has been known to have his plane stop in LA so that he can bring back their burgers.

But in all candor, folks, NYC is a restaurant city that excels at all types of food. But beyond the haute cuisine establishments and looking at everyday fare, Italian food (Little Italy and Arthur Avenue) is top-notch, and Greek and Mediterranean stand out. Of course, NYC's Chinatown food is among the best in this country. NY did not create the diner but has among the best in the country.

With all due respect to the fine Jewish-style delis in the desert, none come close to Katz's on the Lower East Side. And please don't get me started regarding bagels. There are NYC bagels and bagel wannabes elsewhere.

The conclusion, if any, is that dining out is not just about the food. It's about the ambiance, the company you're with, and the experience. I always tell people who go over the top in complaints about a meal—relax. It's not your last one.

# # #

All things considered, I'm reminded of the Neil Diamond song:

> *L.A.'s fine, the sun shines most the time*
>
> *And the feeling is "lay back"*
>
> *Palm trees grow and rents are low*
>
> *But you know I keep thinkin' about*
>
> *Making my way back.*
>
> *Well I'm New York City born and raised*
>
> *But nowadays,*
>
> *I'm lost between two shores*
>
> *L.A.'s fine, but it ain't home*
>
> *New York's home,*
>
> *But it ain't mine no more.*

ACKNOWLEDGMENTS AND THANKS

In keeping with the short story aspect of this book, I will keep this brief.

Any writing journey takes time, patience, and the support of friends and family. This book would not have happened if it were not for the encouragement of my wife, Marlene, who endlessly reviewed my text and offered advice, support, and guidance.

Thank you, Miki Hickel and Hannah Forman, for your support, ideas, encouragement, and hard work in making this happen. Both these wonderful people know their way around self-publishing and were instrumental in making this book happen. Rest up. The next book is coming soon.

To my business partner, Rob Warren, thanks for your support and encouragement.

Our friends and neighbors in Rancho Mirage, California, thanks for answering my silly questions, not least of which had to do with the title—Special thanks to the members of the Writers Forum for your support.

My new and good friend Jim Wobig at Wobig Photography, (wobigphoto.com) thanks for the headshots and photos.

Above all, thank you to the nine million+ residents of New York City. My hometown's 400-year journey, whose adventures, wonders, success, foolishness, and hurdles formed the foundation of these stories.

Printed in the USA
CPSIA information can be obtained
at www.ICGtesting.com
LVHW031208181223
766490LV00090B/3418

9 780997 618129